William James Rolfe, Alfred Tennyson

Select Poems of Alfred Lord Tennyson

Vol. 1

William James Rolfe, Alfred Tennyson

Select Poems of Alfred Lord Tennyson
Vol. 1

ISBN/EAN: 9783337408251

Printed in Europe, USA, Canada, Australia, Japan

Cover: Foto ©Andreas Hilbeck / pixelio.de

More available books at **www.hansebooks.com**

SELECT POEMS

OF

ALFRED LORD TENNYSON

EDITED WITH NOTES

BY

WILLIAM J. ROLFE, A.M.

FORMERLY HEAD MASTER OF THE HIGH SCHOOL, CAMBRIDGE, MASS.

WITH ILLUSTRATIONS

BOSTON

JAMES R. OSGOOD AND COMPANY

1885

University Press:

JOHN WILSON AND SON, CAMBRIDGE.

PREFACE.

THE text of the poems in this volume is that of the last English (1884) edition. For the readings of the editions of 1830, 1832, and 1842, I have had to depend upon quotations in the reviews and in the commentaries of Shepherd, Tainsh, Wace, Bayne, and others. These early editions are not in the Cambridge or Boston libraries, and I have not been able to find them anywhere on this side of the Atlantic. An inquiry for them inserted in the *Literary World* proved as unavailing as the letters I had sent to friends in various parts of the country and in Canada. I did get track of the 1832 volume in several quarters; but all these "trails," when followed up, led to a single copy belonging to Ralph Waldo Emerson, which has recently disappeared from his library and cannot be traced. He lent it, fifty years ago, to many of his friends — among them, Mr. John S. Dwight, who reviewed it in the *Christian Examiner* in 1833, and Mrs. Hawthorne (then Miss Peabody), who made a drawing to illustrate *The Lady of Shalott*.

For the changes in the more recent editions, I have depended mainly on the American reprints, all of which, from 1849 down, I have been able to consult. For the readings of the first edition of the Wellington *Ode*, I used a copy given to the Harvard College Library by Mr. Longfellow.

To explain the omission of certain pieces which are specially appropriate for school and home reading, I may add that many favorite poems suited to a younger class of readers than those for whom the present selection is designed, have been reserved for another volume.

CAMBRIDGE, *August* 9, 1884.

NOTE. — Since the above was in type, Miss Elizabeth Peabody has sent me the following note, which she permits me to print here: —

"If you see Mr. Tennyson in Europe, I wish you would tell him that in correcting the first inspirations of his Muse he made a mistake; that nobody ought to do *that*! The critical understanding is a finite growth in time, but the poetic imagination is a divine influx of the eternal whole that knows better how to use nature's symbols.

" In *The Lady of Shalott* there was, in the first edition, a passage describing the lady ' looking down to Camelot,' that was so wonderful in its effect on the imagination that my sister, Mrs. Nathaniel Hawthorne, drew the figure and face, and the river ruffled by ' the east wind chilly,' in an outline *à la* Flaxman, which completely reproduced the effect of the beautiful lines; but when the second edition came out *the lines were changed*, so that the design was without its archetype. I tried to make my sister send the sketch to Mr. Tennyson, as the best lesson to give him, for I thought *all* his alterations — but especially that one — mistakes. I remember I wrote him a note to go with the sketch, in which I spoke to him of the Dresden Madonna, which was one of those inspirations that so mastered the artist that he always believed the Madonna stood before him with the child — and so never dared to *touch it again*, lest his own shortcoming might put out the light of the original *revelation* that he embodied (? *Nature* with the divine humanity in its arms — looking forward *through* the passion and the cross to the triumph of the resurrection and ascension, which should make all the agony bearable).

" Was not this inspiration something *above* the natural outcome of the *character* Raphael developed on earth? It seems to me to reveal the great law of the supremacy of the Ideal, which the youthful genius of Tennyson so often realized. Wordsworth, as well as Tennyson, seems to me to have profaned in the same way some of the most wonderful expressions of the absolute Ideal vouchsafed to him — for instance, in one line of his *Ode to Duty*, in which the scientific theologian presumes to correct the inspired prophet.

" My sister was so modest I never could persuade her to send the sketch, and so my note did not go, and now both are lost. When I went to England in 1871, on news of her death, I could not find them among her papers, or would have sent them then."

CONTENTS.

' Courage,' he said, and pointed toward the land,
' This mounting wave will roll us shoreward soon.'

The Lotos-Eaters.

SELECT POEMS

OF

ALFRED LORD TENNYSON.

RECOLLECTIONS OF THE ARABIAN NIGHTS.

WHEN the breeze of a joyful dawn blew free
   In the silken sail of infancy,
The tide of time flow'd back with me,
   The forward-flowing tide of time;
And many a sheeny summer morn,
Adown the Tigris I was borne,
By Bagdat's shrines of fretted gold,
High-walled gardens green and old.
True Mussulman was I and sworn,
   For it was in the golden prime
     Of good Haroun Alraschid.

Anight my shallop, rustling thro'
The low and bloomed foliage, drove
The fragrant, glistening deeps, and clove
The citron-shadows in the blue ;
By garden porches on the brim,
The costly doors flung open wide,
Gold glittering thro' lamp-light dim,
And broider'd sofas on each side.
    In sooth it was a goodly time,
    For it was in the golden prime
        Of good Haroun Alraschid.

Often, where clear-stemm'd platans guard
The outlet, did I turn away
The boat-head down a broad canal
From the main river sluiced, where all
The sloping of the moon-lit sward
Was damask-work, and deep inlay
Of braided blooms unmown, which crept
Adown to where the water slept.
    A goodly place, a goodly time,
    For it was in the golden prime
        Of good Haroun Alraschid.

A motion from the river won
Ridged the smooth level, bearing on
My shallop thro' the star-strown calm,
Until another night in night
I enter'd, from the clearer light,
Imbower'd vaults of pillar'd palm,
Imprisoning sweets, which, as they clomb
Heavenward, were stay'd beneath the dome
    Of hollow boughs.   A goodly time,
    For it was in the golden prime
        Of good Haroun Alraschid.

Still onward ; and the clear canal
Is rounded to as clear a lake.
From the green rivage many a fall
Of diamond rillets musical,
Thro' little crystal arches low
Down from the central fountain's flow   50
Fallen silver-chiming, seem'd to shake
The sparkling flints beneath the prow.
   A goodly place, a goodly time,
   For it was in the golden prime
     Of good Haroun Alraschid.

Above thro' many a bowery turn
A walk with vary-color'd shells
Wander'd engrain'd. On either side
All round about the fragrant marge
From fluted vase, and brazen urn   60
In order, eastern flowers large,
Some dropping low their crimson bells
Half-closed, and others studded wide
   With disks and tiars, fed the time
   With odor in the golden prime
     Of good Haroun Alraschid.

Far off, and where the lemon grove
In closest coverture upsprung,
The living airs of middle night
Died round the bulbul as he sung ;   70
Not he, but something which possess'd
The darkness of the world, delight,
Life, anguish, death, immortal love,
Ceasing not, mingled, unrepress'd,
   Apart from place, withholding time,
   But flattering the golden prime
     Of good Haroun Alraschid.

Black the garden-bowers and grots
Slumber'd; the solemn palms were ranged
Above, unwoo'd of summer wind;
A sudden splendor from behind
Flush'd all the leaves with rich gold-green,
And, flowing rapidly between
Their interspaces, counterchanged
The level lake with diamond-plots
   Of dark and bright.   A lovely time,
    For it was in the golden prime
      Of good Haroun Alraschid.

Dark-blue the deep sphere overhead,
Distinct with vivid stars inlaid,
Grew darker from that under-flame;
So, leaping lightly from the boat,
With silver anchor left afloat,
In marvel whence that glory came
Upon me, as in sleep I sank
In cool soft turf upon the bank,
   Entranced with that place and time,
    So worthy of the golden prime
      Of good Haroun Alraschid.

Thence thro' the garden I was drawn —
A realm of pleasance, many a mound,
And many a shadow-chequer'd lawn
Full of the city's stilly sound,
And deep myrrh-thickets blowing round
The stately cedar, tamarisks,
Thick rosaries of scented thorn,
Tall orient shrubs, and obelisks
   Graven with emblems of the time,
    In honor of the golden prime
      Of good Haroun Alraschid.

With dazed vision unawares
From the long alley's latticed shade
Emerged, I came upon the great
Pavilion of the Caliphat.
Right to the carven cedarn doors,
Flung inward over spangled floors,
Broad-based flights of marble stairs
Ran up with golden balustrade,
   After the fashion of the time,
   And humor of the golden prime   120
      Of good Haroun Alraschid.

The fourscore windows all alight
As with the quintessence of flame,
A million tapers flaring bright
From twisted silvers look'd to shame
The hollow-vaulted dark, and stream'd
Upon the mooned domes aloof
In inmost Bagdat, till there seem'd
Hundreds of crescents on the roof
   Of night new-risen, that marvellous time,   130
   To celebrate the golden prime
      Of good Haroun Alraschid.

Then stole I up, and trancedly
Gazed on the Persian girl alone,
Serene with argent-lidded eyes
Amorous, and lashes like to rays
Of darkness, and a brow of pearl
Tressed with redolent ebony,
In many a dark delicious curl,
Flowing beneath her rose-hued zone ;   140
   The sweetest lady of the time,
   Well worthy of the golden prime
      Of good Haroun Alraschid.

Six columns, three on either side,
Pure silver, underpropt a rich
Throne of the massive ore, from which
Down droop'd in many a floating fold,
Engarlanded and diaper'd
With inwrought flowers, a cloth of gold.
Thereon, his deep eye laughter-stirr'd   150
With merriment of kingly pride,
   Sole star of all that place and time,
   I saw him — in his golden prime,
     THE GOOD HAROUN ALRASCHID !

THE POET.

THE poet in a golden clime was born,
   With golden stars above ;
Dower'd with the hate of hate, the scorn of scorn,
   The love of love.

He saw thro' life and death, thro' good and ill,
　　He saw thro' his own soul.
The marvel of the everlasting will,
　　An open scroll,

Before him lay : with echoing feet he threaded
　　The secretest walks of fame :　　　　10
The viewless arrows of his thoughts were headed
　　And wing'd with flame,

Like Indian reeds blown from his silver tongue,
　　And of so fierce a flight,
From Calpe unto Caucasus they sung,
　　Filling with light

And vagrant melodies the winds which bore
　　Them earthward till they lit ;
Then, like the arrow-seeds of the field flower,
　　The fruitful wit　　　　20

Cleaving took root, and springing forth anew
　　Where'er they fell, behold,
Like to the mother plant in semblance, grew
　　A flower all gold,

And bravely furnish'd all abroad to fling
　　The winged shafts of truth,
To throng with stately blooms the breathing spring
　　Of Hope and Youth.

So many minds did gird their orbs with beams,
　　Tho' one did fling the fire.　　　　30
Heaven flow'd upon the soul in many dreams
　　Of high desire.

Thus truth was multiplied on truth, the world
    Like one great garden show'd,
And thro' the wreaths of floating dark upcurl'd,
    Rare sunrise flow'd.

And Freedom rear'd in that august sunrise
    Her beautiful bold brow,
When rites and forms before his burning eyes
    Melted like snow.   40

There was no blood upon her maiden robes
    Sunn'd by those orient skies ;
But round about the circles of the globes
    Of her keen eyes

And in her raiment's hem was traced in flame
    WISDOM, a name to shake
All evil dreams of power — a sacred name.
    And when she spake,

Her words did gather thunder as they ran,
    And as the lightning to the thunder   50
Which follows it, riving the spirit of man,
    Making earth wonder,

So was their meaning to her words.   No sword
    Of wrath her right arm whirl'd,
But one poor poet's scroll, and with *his* word
    She shook the world.

THE LADY OF SHALOTT.

PART I.

ON either side the river lie
Long fields of barley and of rye,
That clothe the wold and meet the sky;
And thro' the field the road runs by
      To many-tower'd Camelot;

And up and down the people go,
Gazing where the lilies blow
Round an island there below,
     The island of Shalott.

Willows whiten, aspens quiver,
Little breezes dusk and shiver
Thro' the wave that runs forever
By the island in the river
     Flowing down to Camelot.
Four gray walls, and four gray towers,
Overlook a space of flowers,
And the silent isle imbowers
     The Lady of Shalott.

By the margin, willow-veil'd,
Slide the heavy barges trail'd
By slow horses; and unhail'd
The shallop flitteth silken-sail'd
     Skimming down to Camelot:
But who hath seen her wave her hand?
Or at the casement seen her stand?
Or is she known in all the land,
     The Lady of Shalott?

Only reapers, reaping early
In among the bearded barley,
Hear a song that echoes cheerly
From the river winding clearly,
     Down to tower'd Camelot:
And by the moon the reaper weary,
Piling sheaves in uplands airy,
Listening, whispers, ''T is the fairy
     Lady of Shalott.'

PART II.

THERE she weaves by night and day
A magic web with colors gay.
She has heard a whisper say,
A curse is on her if she stay
      To look down to Camelot.
She knows not what the curse may be,
And so she weaveth steadily,
And little other care hath she,
      The Lady of Shalott.

And moving thro' a mirror clear
That hangs before her all the year,
Shadows of the world appear.
There she sees the highway near
      Winding down to Camelot;
There the river eddy whirls,
And there the surly village-churls,
And the red cloaks of market girls,
      Pass onward from Shalott.

Sometimes a troop of damsels glad,
An abbot on an ambling pad,
Sometimes a curly shepherd-lad,
Or long-hair'd page in crimson clad,
      Goes by to tower'd Camelot;
And sometimes thro' the mirror blue
The knights come riding two and two:
She hath no loyal knight and true,
      The Lady of Shalott.

But in her web she still delights
To weave the mirror's magic sights,

For often thro' the silent nights
A funeral, with plumes and lights
      And music, went to Camelot:
Or when the moon was overhead,
Came two young lovers lately wed;
'I am half-sick of shadows,' said
      The Lady of Shalott.

PART III.

A BOW-SHOT from her bower-eaves,
He rode between the barley-sheaves;
The sun came dazzling thro' the leaves,
And flamed upon the brazen greaves
      Of bold Sir Lancelot.
A red-cross knight forever kneel'd
To a lady in his shield,
That sparkled on the yellow field,
      Beside remote Shalott.

The gemmy bridle glitter'd free,
Like to some branch of stars we see
Hung in the golden Galaxy.
The bridle bells rang merrily
      As he rode down to Camelot;
And from his blazon'd baldric slung
A mighty silver bugle hung,
And as he rode his armor rung,
      Beside remote Shalott.

All in the blue unclouded weather
Thick-jewell'd shone the saddle-leather,
The helmet and the helmet-feather
Burn'd like one burning flame together,
      As he rode down to Camelot;

As often thro' the purple night,
Below the starry clusters bright,
Some bearded meteor, trailing light,
   Moves over still Shalott.

His broad clear brow in sunlight glow'd ;   100
On burnish'd hooves his war-horse trode ;
From underneath his helmet flow'd
His coal-black curls as on he rode,
   As he rode down to Camelot.
From the bank and from the river
He flash'd into the crystal mirror ;
'Tirra lirra,' by the river
   Sang Sir Lancelot.

She left the web, she left the loom,
She made three paces thro' the room,   110
She saw the water-lily bloom,
She saw the helmet and the plume,
   She look'd down to Camelot.
Out flew the web and floated wide ;
The mirror crack'd from side to side :
'The curse has come upon me,' cried
   The Lady of Shalott.

PART IV.

IN the stormy east-wind straining,
The pale yellow woods were waning,
The broad stream in his banks complaining,   120
Heavily the low sky raining
   Over tower'd Camelot ;
Down she came and found a boat
Beneath a willow left afloat,
And round about the prow she wrote
   The Lady of Shalott.

And down the river's dim expanse —
Like some bold seer in a trance,
Seeing all his own mischance —
With a glassy countenance
      Did she look to Camelot.
And at the closing of the day
She loosed the chain, and down she lay;
The broad stream bore her far away,
      The Lady of Shalott.

Lying, robed in snowy white
That loosely flew to left and right —
The leaves upon her falling light —
Thro' the noises of the night
      She floated down to Camelot;
And as the boat-head wound along
The willowy hills and fields among,
They heard her singing her last song,
      The Lady of Shalott.

Heard a carol, mournful, holy,
Chanted loudly, chanted lowly,
Till her blood was frozen slowly,
And her eyes were darken'd wholly,
      Turn'd to tower'd Camelot;
For ere she reach'd upon the tide
The first house by the water-side,
Singing in her song she died,
      The Lady of Shalott.

Under tower and balcony,
By garden-wall and gallery,
A gleaming shape she floated by,
Dead-pale between the houses high,
      Silent into Camelot.

Out upon the wharfs they came,
Knight and burgher, lord and dame,   160
And round the prow they read her name,
    The Lady of Shalott.

Who is this? and what is here?
And in the lighted palace near
Died the sound of royal cheer;
And they cross'd themselves for fear,
      All the knights at Camelot:
But Lancelot mused a little space;
He said, 'She has a lovely face;
God in his mercy lend her grace,   170
    The Lady of Shalott.'

THE MILLER'S DAUGHTER.

I SEE the wealthy miller yet,
  His double chin, his portly size,
And who that knew him could forget
  The busy wrinkles round his eyes?

The slow wise smile that, round about
    His dusty forehead drily curl'd,
Seem'd half-within and half-without,
    And full of dealings with the world?

In yonder chair I see him sit,
    Three fingers round the old silver cup —   10
I see his gray eyes twinkle yet
    At his own jest — gray eyes lit up
With summer lightnings of a soul
    So full of summer warmth, so glad,
So healthy, sound, and clear and whole,
    His memory scarce can make me sad.

Yet fill my glass : give me one kiss :
    My own sweet Alice, we must die.
There's somewhat in this world amiss
    Shall be unriddled by and by.   20
There's somewhat flows to us in life,
    But more is taken quite away.
Pray, Alice, pray, my darling wife,
    That we may die the selfsame day.

Have I not found a happy earth?
    I least should breathe a thought of pain.
Would God renew me from my birth,
    I 'd almost live my life again.
So sweet it seems with thee to walk,
    And once again to woo thee mine —   30
It seems in after-dinner talk
    Across the walnuts and the wine —

To be the long and listless boy
    Late-left an orphan of the squire,
Where this old mansion mounted high
    Looks down upon the village spire ;

For even here, where I and you
   Have lived and loved alone so long,
Each morn my sleep was broken thro'
   By some wild skylark's matin song.   40

And oft I heard the tender dove
   In firry woodlands making moan ;
But ere I saw your eyes, my love,
   I had no motion of my own.
For scarce my life with fancy play'd
   Before I dream'd that pleasant dream —
Still hither thither idly sway'd
   Like those long mosses in the stream.

Or from the bridge I lean'd to hear
   The mill-dam rushing down with noise,   50
And see the minnows everywhere
   In crystal eddies glance and poise,
The tall flag-flowers when they sprung
   Below the range of stepping-stones,
Or those three chestnuts near, that hung
   In masses thick with milky cones.

But, Alice, what an hour was that,
   When after roving in the woods
('T was April then), I came and sat
   Below the chestnuts, when their buds   60
Were glistening to the breezy blue ;
   And on the slope, an absent fool,
I cast me down, nor thought of you,
   But angled in the higher pool.

A love-song I had somewhere read,
   An echo from a measured strain,
Beat time to nothing in my head
   From some odd corner of the brain.

It haunted me, the morning long,
   With weary sameness in the rhymes,   70
The phantom of a silent song,
   That went and came a thousand times.

Then leapt a trout. In lazy mood
   I watch'd the little circles die ;
They past into the level flood,
   And there a vision caught my eye ;
The reflex of a beauteous form,
   A glowing arm, a gleaming neck,
As when a sunbeam wavers warm
   Within the dark and dimpled beck.   80

For you remember, you had set,
   That morning, on the casement-edge
A long green box of mignonette,
   And you were leaning from the ledge ;
And when I raised my eyes, above
   They met with two so full and bright —
Such eyes ! I swear to you, my love,
   That these have never lost their light.

I loved, and love dispell'd the fear
   That I should die an early death ;   90
For love possess'd the atmosphere,
   And fill'd the breast with purer breath.
My mother thought, What ails the boy?
   For I was alter'd, and began
To move about the house with joy,
   And with the certain step of man.

I loved the brimming wave that swam
   Thro' quiet meadows round the mill,
The sleepy pool above the dam,
   The pool beneath it never still,   100

The meal-sacks on the whiten'd floor,
　　The dark round of the dripping wheel,
The very air about the door
　　Made misty with the floating meal.

And oft in ramblings on the wold,
　　When April nights began to blow,
And April's crescent glimmer'd cold,
　　I saw the village lights below;
I knew your taper far away,
　　And full at heart of trembling hope,　　　　110
From off the wold I came, and lay
　　Upon the freshly-flower'd slope.

The deep brook groan'd beneath the mill;
　　And 'by that lamp,' I thought, 'she sits!'
The white chalk-quarry from the hill
　　Gleamed to the flying moon by fits.
'O that I were beside her now!
　　O will she answer if I call?
O would she give me vow for vow,
　　Sweet Alice, if I told her all?'　　　　120

Sometimes I saw you sit and spin;
　　And, in the pauses of the wind,
Sometimes I heard you sing within;
　　Sometimes your shadow cross'd the blind.
At last you rose and moved the light,
　　And the long shadow of the chair
Flitted across into the night,
　　And all the casement darken'd there.

But when at last I dared to speak,
　　The lanes, you know, were white with may;　　130
Your ripe lips moved not, but your cheek
　　Flush'd like the coming of the day:

And so it was — half-sly, half-shy,
  You would, and would not, little one !
Although I pleaded tenderly,
  And you and I were all alone.

And slowly was my mother brought
  To yield consent to my desire :
She wish'd me happy, but she thought
  I might have look'd a little higher ;   140
And I was young — too young to wed :
  'Yet must I love her for your sake ;
Go fetch your Alice here,' she said :
  Her eyelid quiver'd as she spake.

And down I went to fetch my bride :
  But, Alice, you were ill at ease ;
This dress and that by turns you tried,
  Too fearful that you should not please.
I loved you better for your fears,
  I knew you could not look but well ;   150
And dews, that would have fallen in tears,
  I kiss'd away before they fell.

I watch'd the little flutterings,
  The doubt my mother would not see ;
She spoke at large of many things,
  And at the last she spoke of me ;
And turning look'd upon your face,
  As near this door you sat apart,
And rose, and, with a silent grace
  Approaching, press'd you heart to heart.   160

Ah, well — but sing the foolish song
  I gave you, Alice, on the day
When, arm in arm, we went along,
  A pensive pair, and you were gay

With bridal flowers — that I may seem,
  As in the nights of old, to lie
Beside the mill-wheel in the stream,
  While those full chestnuts whisper by.

    It is the miller's daughter,
      And she is grown so dear, so dear,   170
    That I would be the jewel
      That trembles at her ear;
    For hid in ringlets day and night,
    I 'd touch her neck so warm and white.

    And I would be the girdle
      About her dainty, dainty waist,
    And her heart would beat against me,
      In sorrow and in rest;
    And I should know if it beat right,
    I 'd clasp it round so close and tight.   180

    And I would be the necklace,
      And all day long to fall and rise
    Upon her balmy bosom,
      With her laughter or her sighs;
    And I would lie so light, so light,
    I scarce should be unclasp'd at night.

A trifle, sweet ! which true love spells —
  True love interprets — right alone. ·
His light upon the letter dwells,
  For all the spirit is his own.   190
So, if I waste words now, in truth,
  You must blame Love.   His early rage
Had force to make me rhyme in youth,
  And makes me talk too much in age.

And now those vivid hours are gone,
  Like mine own life to me thou art,
Where Past and Present, wound in one,
  Do make a garland for the heart :

So sing that other song I made,
    Half-anger'd with my happy lot,
The day, when in the chestnut-shade
    I found the blue forget-me-not.

      Love that hath us in the net.
      Can he pass, and we forget?
      Many suns arise and set.
      Many a chance the years beget.
      Love the gift is Love the debt.
          Even so.

      Love is hurt with jar and fret.
      Love is made a vague regret.
      Eyes with idle tears are wet.
      Idle habit links us yet.
      What is love? for we forget:
          Ah, no! no!

Look thro' mine eyes with thine.   True wife,
    Round my true heart thine arms entwine;
My other dearer life in life,
    Look thro' my very soul with thine!
Untouch'd with any shade of years,
    May those kind eyes forever dwell!
They have not shed a many tears,
    Dear eyes, since first I knew them well.

Yet tears they shed; they had their part
    Of sorrow: for when time was ripe,
The still affection of the heart
    Became an outward breathing type,
That into stillness past again,
    And left a want unknown before;
Although the loss had brought us pain,
    That loss but made us love the more,

With farther lookings on.   The kiss,
    The woven arms, seem but to be
Weak symbols of the settled bliss,
    The comfort, I have found in thee :
But that God bless thee, dear — who wrought
    Two spirits to one equal mind —
With blessings beyond hope or thought,
    With blessings which no words can find.

Arise, and let us wander forth,
    To yon old mill across the wolds ;   240
For look, the sunset, south and north,
    Winds all the vale in rosy folds,
And fires your narrow casement glass,
    Touching the sullen pool below :
On the chalk-hill the bearded grass
    Is dry and dewless.   Let us go.

ŒNONE.

THERE lies a vale in Ida, lovelier
Than all the valleys of Ionian hills.
The swimming vapor slopes athwart the glen,
Puts forth an arm, and creeps from pine to pine,

And loiters, slowly drawn.   On either hand
The lawns and meadow-ledges midway down
Hang rich in flowers, and far below them roars
The long brook falling thro' the cloven ravine
In cataract after cataract to the sea.
Behind the valley topmost Gargarus   10
Stands up and takes the morning; but in front
The gorges, opening wide apart, reveal
Troas and Ilion's column'd citadel,
The crown of Troas.
      Hither came at noon
Mournful Œnone, wandering forlorn
Of Paris, once her playmate on the hills.
Her cheek had lost the rose, and round her neck
Floated her hair or seem'd to float in rest.
She, leaning on a fragment twined with vine,
Sang to the stillness, till the mountain-shade   20
Sloped downward to her seat from the upper cliff.

'O mother Ida, many-fountain'd Ida,
Dear mother Ida, hearken ere I die.
For now the noonday quiet holds the hill;
The grasshopper is silent in the grass;
The lizard, with his shadow on the stone,
Rests like a shadow, and the winds are dead.
The purple flower droops; the golden bee
Is lily-cradled: I alone awake.
My eyes are full of tears, my heart of love,   30
My heart is breaking, and my eyes are dim,
And I am all aweary of my life.

'O mother Ida, many-fountain'd Ida,
Dear mother Ida, hearken ere I die.
Hear me, O earth, hear me, O hills, O caves
That house the cold crown'd snake! O mountain brooks,

I am the daughter of a River-God,
Hear me, for I will speak, and build up all
My sorrow with my song, as yonder walls
Rose slowly to a music slowly breathed,   40
A cloud that gather'd shape ; for it may be
That, while I speak of it, a little while
My heart may wander from its deeper woe.

   ' O mother Ida, many-fountain'd Ida,
Dear mother Ida, hearken ere I die.
I waited underneath the dawning hills ;
Aloft the mountain lawn was dewy-dark,
And dewy-dark aloft the mountain pine :
Beautiful Paris, evil-hearted Paris,
Leading a jet-black goat white-horn'd, white-hooved,   50
Came up from reedy Simois all alone.

   ' O mother Ida, hearken ere I die.
Far-off the torrent call'd me from the cleft ;
Far up the solitary morning smote
The streaks of virgin snow.   With down-dropt eyes
I sat alone : white-breasted like a star
Fronting the dawn he moved ; a leopard skin
Droop'd from his shoulder, but his sunny hair
Cluster'd about his temples like a God's ;
And his cheek brighten'd as the foam-bow brightens   60
When the wind blows the foam, and all my heart
Went forth to embrace him coming ere he came.

   ' Dear mother Ida, hearken ere I die.
He smiled, and opening out his milk-white palm
Disclosed a fruit of pure Hesperian gold,
That smelt ambrosially, and while I look'd
And listen'd, the full-flowing river of speech
Came down upon my heart.

                                              " My own Œnone,
Beautiful-brow'd Œnone, my own soul,
Behold this fruit, whose gleaming rind ingraven   70
' For the most fair,' would seem to award it thine,
As lovelier than whatever Oread haunt
The knolls of Ida, loveliest in all grace
Of movement, and the charm of married brows."

       ' Dear mother Ida, hearken ere I die.
He prest the blossom of his lips to mine,
And added, " This was cast upon the board,
When all the full-faced presence of the Gods
Ranged in the halls of Peleus ; whereupon
Rose feud, with question unto whom 't were due :   80
But light-foot Iris brought it yester-eve,
Delivering, that to me, by common voice
Elected umpire, Herè comes to-day,
Pallas and Aphrodite, claiming each
This meed of fairest.   Thou, within the cave
Behind yon whispering tuft of oldest pine,
Mayst well behold them unbeheld, unheard
Hear all, and see thy Paris judge of Gods."

       ' Dear mother Ida, hearken ere I die.
It was the deep midnoon ; one silvery cloud   90
Had lost his way between the piny sides
Of this long glen.   Then to the bower they came,
Naked they came to that smooth-swarded bower,
And at their feet the crocus brake like fire,
Violet, amaracus, and asphodel,
Lotos and lilies ; and a wind arose,
And overhead the wandering ivy and vine,
This way and that, in many a wild festoon
Ran riot, garlanding the gnarled boughs
With bunch and berry and flower thro' and thro'.   100

'O mother Ida, hearken ere I die.
On the tree-tops a crested peacock lit,
And o'er him flow'd a golden cloud, and lean'd
Upon him, slowly dropping fragrant dew.
Then first I heard the voice of her, to whom
Coming thro' heaven, like a light that grows
Larger and clearer, with one mind the Gods
Rise.up for reverence. She to Paris made
Proffer of royal power, ample rule
Unquestion'd, overflowing revenue   110
Wherewith to embellish state, "from many a vale
And river-sunder'd champaign clothed with corn,
Or labor'd mine undrainable of ore.
Honor," she said, "and homage, tax and toll,
From many an inland town and haven large,
Mast-throng'd beneath her shadowing citadel
In glassy bays among her tallest towers."

'O mother Ida, hearken ere I die.
Still she spake on and still she spake of power,
"Which in all action is the end of all ;   120
Power fitted to the season ; wisdom-bred
And throned of wisdom — from all neighbor crowns
Alliance and allegiance, till thy hand
Fail from the sceptre-staff. Such boon from me,
From me, heaven's queen, Paris, to thee king-born,
A shepherd all thy life but yet king-born,
Should come most welcome, seeing men, in power
Only, are likest Gods, who have attain'd
Rest in a happy place and quiet seats
Above the thunder, with undying bliss   130
In knowledge of their own supremacy."

'Dear mother Ida, hearken ere I die.
She ceased, and Paris held the costly fruit

Out at arm's-length, so much the thought of power
Flatter'd his spirit ; but Pallas where she stood
Somewhat apart, her clear and bared limbs
O'erthwarted with the brazen-headed spear
Upon her pearly shoulder leaning cold,
The while, above, her full and earnest eye
Over her snow-cold breast and angry cheek   140
Kept watch, waiting decision, made reply.

   ' " Self-reverence, self-knowledge, self-control,
These three alone lead life to sovereign power.
Yet not for power (power of herself
Would come uncall'd for), but to live by law,
Acting the law we live by without fear ;
And, because right is right, to follow right
Were wisdom in the scorn of consequence."

   ' Dear mother Ida, hearken ere I die.
Again she said : " I woo thee not with gifts.   150
Sequel of guerdon could not alter me
To fairer.   Judge thou me by what I am,
So shalt thou find me fairest.
                         Yet, indeed,
If gazing on divinity disrobed
Thy mortal eyes are frail to judge of fair,
Unbiass'd by self-profit, oh ! rest thee sure
That I shall love thee well and cleave to thee,
So that my vigor, wedded to thy blood,
Shall strike within thy pulses, like a God's,
To push thee forward thro' a life of shocks,   160
Dangers, and deeds, until endurance grow
Sinew'd with action, and the full-grown will,
Circled thro' all experiences, pure law,
Commeasure perfect freedom."

Here she ceased,
And Paris ponder'd, and I cried, " O Paris,
Give it to Pallas ! " but he heard me not,
Or hearing would not hear me, woe is me !

' O mother Ida, many-fountain'd Ida,
Dear mother Ida, hearken ere I die.
Idalian Aphrodite beautiful,   170
Fresh as the foam, new-bathed in Paphian wells,
With rosy slender fingers backward drew
From her warm brows and bosom her deep hair
Ambrosial, golden round her lucid throat
And shoulder ; from the violets her light foot
Shone rosy-white, and o'er her rounded form
Between the shadows of the vine-bunches
Floated the glowing sunlights, as she moved.

' Dear mother Ida, hearken ere I die.
She with a subtle smile in her mild eyes,   180
The herald of her triumph, drawing nigh
Half-whisper'd in his ear, " I promise thee
The fairest and most loving wife in Greece."
She spoke and laugh'd ; I shut my sight for fear.
But when I look'd, Paris had raised his arm,
And I beheld great Herè's angry eyes,
As she withdrew into the golden cloud,
And I was left alone within the bower ;
And from that time to this I am alone,
And I shall be alone until I die.   190

' Yet, mother Ida, hearken ere I die.
Fairest — why fairest wife ? am I not fair ?
My love hath told me so a thousand times.
Methinks I must be fair, for yesterday,
When I past by, a wild and wanton pard,
Eyed like the evening star, with playful tail
Crouch'd fawning in the weed.   Most loving is she ?

Ah me, my mountain shepherd, that my arms
Were wound about thee, and my hot lips prest
Close, close to thine in that quick-falling dew   200
Of fruitful kisses, thick as Autumn rains
Flash in the pools of whirling Simois !

    ' O mother, hear me yet before I die.
They came, they cut away my tallest pines,
My dark tall pines, that plumed the craggy ledge
High over the blue gorge, and all between
The snowy peak and snow-white cataract
Foster'd the callow eaglet — from beneath
Whose thick mysterious boughs in the dark morn
The panther's roar came muffled, while I sat   210
Low in the valley.   Never, never more
Shall lone Œnone see the morning mist
Sweep thro' them ; never see them overlaid
With narrow moon-lit slips of silver cloud,
Between the loud stream and the trembling stars.

    ' O mother, hear me yet before I die.
I wish that somewhere in the ruin'd folds,
Among the fragments tumbled from the glens,
Or the dry thickets, I could meet with her,
The Abominable, that uninvited came   220
Into the fair Peleïan banquet-hall,
And cast the golden fruit upon the board,
And bred this change ; that I might speak my mind,
And tell her to her face how much I hate
Her presence, hated both of Gods and men.

    ' O mother, hear me yet before I die.
Hath he not sworn his love a thousand times,
In this green valley, under this green hill,
Even on this hand, and sitting on this stone ?
Seal'd it with kisses ? water'd it with tears ?   230

O happy tears, and how unlike to these !
O happy heaven, how canst thou see my face?
O happy earth, how canst thou bear my weight?
O death, death, death, thou ever-floating cloud,
There are enough unhappy on this earth,
Pass by the happy souls, that love to live ;
I pray thee, pass before my light of life,
And shadow all my soul, that I may die.
Thou weighest heavy on the heart within,
Weigh heavy on my eyelids ; let me die.   240

  'O mother, hear me yet before I die.
I will not die alone, for fiery thoughts
Do shape themselves within me, more and more,
Whereof I catch the issue, as I hear
Dead sounds at night come from the inmost hills,
Like footsteps upon wool.   I dimly see
My far-off doubtful purpose, as a mother
Conjectures of the features of her child
Ere it is born : her child ! — a shudder comes
Across me : never child be born of me,   250
Unblest, to vex me with his father's eyes !

  'O mother, hear me yet before I die.
Hear me, O earth.   I will not die alone,
Lest their shrill happy laughter come to me
Walking the cold and starless road of death
Uncomforted, leaving my ancient love
With the Greek woman.   I will rise and go
Down into Troy, and ere the stars come forth
Talk with the wild Cassandra, for she says
A fire dances before her, and a sound   260
Rings ever in her ears of armed men.
What this may be I know not, but I know
That, wheresoe'er I am by night and day,
All earth and air seem only burning fire.'

THE LOTOS-EATERS.

'Courage!' he said, and pointed toward the land,
'This mounting wave will roll us shoreward soon.'
In the afternoon they came unto a land
In which it seemed always afternoon.
All round the coast the languid air did swoon,
Breathing like one that hath a weary dream.
Full-faced above the valley stood the moon;
And, like a downward smoke, the slender stream
Along the cliff to fall and pause and fall did seem.

A land of streams! some, like a downward smoke,
Slow-dropping veils of thinnest lawn, did go;
And some thro' wavering lights and shadows broke,
Rolling a slumberous sheet of foam below.
They saw the gleaming river seaward flow
From the inner land: far off, three mountain-tops,
Three silent pinnacles of aged snow,
Stood sunset-flush'd; and, dew'd with showery drops,
Up-clomb the shadowy pine above the woven copse.

The charmed sunset linger'd low adown
In the red West: thro' mountain clefts the dale

Was seen far inland, and the yellow down
Border'd with palm, and many a winding vale
And meadow, set with slender galingale ;
A land where all things always seem'd the same !
And round about the keel with faces pale,
Dark faces pale against that rosy flame,
The mild-eyed melancholy Lotos-eaters came.

Branches they bore of that enchanted stem,
Laden with flower and fruit, whereof they gave
To each ; but whoso did receive of them   30
And taste, to him the gushing of the wave
Far far away did seem to mourn and rave
On alien shores ; and if his fellow spake,
His voice was thin, as voices from the grave ;
And deep-asleep he seem'd, yet all awake,
And music in his ears his beating heart did make.

They sat them down upon the yellow sand,
Between the sun and moon upon the shore ;
And sweet it was to dream of Fatherland,
Of child, and wife, and slave ; but evermore   40
Most weary seem'd the sea, weary the oar,
Weary the wandering fields of barren foam.
Then some one said, ' We will return no more ;'
And all at once they sang, ' Our island home
Is far beyond the wave ; we will no longer roam.'

CHORIC SONG.

I.

THERE is sweet music here that softer falls
Than petals from blown roses on the grass,
Or night-dews on still waters between walls
Of shadowy granite, in a gleaming pass ;

Music that gentlier on the spirit lies,
Than tired eyelids upon tired eyes ;
Music that brings sweet sleep down from the blissful skies.
Here are cool mosses deep,
And thro' the moss the ivies creep,
And in the stream the long-leaved flowers weep,
And from the craggy ledge the poppy hangs in sleep.

II.

Why are we weigh'd upon with heaviness,
And utterly consumed with sharp distress,
While all things else have rest from weariness?
All things have rest : why should we toil alone,
We only toil, who are the first of things,
And make perpetual moan,
Still from one sorrow to another thrown ;
Nor ever fold our wings,
And cease from wanderings,
Nor steep our brows in slumber's holy balm ;
Nor hearken what the inner spirit sings,
' There is no joy but calm ! '
Why should we only toil, the roof and crown of things?

III.

Lo ! in the middle of the wood,
The folded leaf is woo'd from out the bud
With winds upon the branch, and there
Grows green and broad, and takes no care,
Sun-steep'd at noon, and in the moon
Nightly dew-fed ; and turning yellow
Falls, and floats adown the air.
Lo ! sweeten'd with the summer light,
The full-juiced apple, waxing over-mellow,
Drops in a silent autumn night.

All its allotted length of days,   80
The flower ripens in its place,
Ripens and fades, and falls, and hath no toil,
Fast-rooted in the fruitful soil.

IV.

Hateful is the dark-blue sky,
Vaulted o'er the dark-blue sea.
Death is the end of life ; ah, why
Should life all labor be?
Let us alone.   Time driveth onward fast,
And in a little while our lips are dumb.
Let us alone.   What is it that will last?   90
All things are taken from us, and become
Portions and parcels of the dreadful Past.
Let us alone.   What pleasure can we have
To war with evil?   Is there any peace
In ever climbing up the climbing wave?
All things have rest, and ripen toward the grave
In silence ; ripen, fall, and cease :
Give us long rest or death, dark death or dreamful ease.

V.

How sweet it were, hearing the downward stream,
With half-shut eyes ever to seem   100
Falling asleep in a half-dream !
To dream and dream, like yonder amber light,
Which will not leave the myrrh-bush on the height ;
To hear each other's whisper'd speech ;
Eating the Lotos day by day,
To watch the crisping ripples on the beach,
And tender curving lines of creamy spray ;
To lend our hearts and spirits wholly
To the influence of mild-minded melancholy ;

To muse and brood and live again in memory
With those old faces of our infancy
Heap'd over with a mound of grass,
Two handfuls of white dust, shut in an urn of brass !

VI.

Dear is the memory of our wedded lives,
And dear the last embraces of our wives
And their warm tears ; but all hath suffer'd change :
For surely now our household hearths are cold ;
Our sons inherit us ; our looks are strange ;
And we should come like ghosts to trouble joy.
Or else the island princes over-bold
Have eat our substance, and the minstrel sings
Before them of the ten years' war in Troy,
And our great deeds, as half-forgotten things.
Is there confusion in the little isle ?
Let what is broken so remain.
The Gods are hard to reconcile ;
'T is hard to settle order once again.
There *is* confusion worse than death,
Trouble on trouble, pain on pain,
Long labor unto aged breath,
Sore task to hearts worn out by many wars,
And eyes grown dim with gazing on the pilot-stars.

VII.

But, propt on beds of amaranth and moly,
How sweet (while warm airs lull us, blowing lowly)
With half-dropt eyelid still,
Beneath a heaven dark and holy,
To watch the long bright river drawing slowly
His waters from the purple hill —
To hear the dewy echoes calling
From cave to cave thro' the thick-twined vine —

To watch the emerald-color'd water falling
Thro' many a woven acanthus-wreath divine !
Only to hear and see the far-off sparkling brine,
Only to hear were sweet, stretch'd out beneath the pine.

VIII.

The Lotos blooms below the barren peak ;
The Lotos blows by every winding creek ;
All day the wind breathes low with mellower tone ;
Thro' every hollow cave and alley lone
Round and round the spicy downs the yellow Lotos-dust is
    blown.
We have had enough of action, and of motion we,   150
Roll'd to starboard, roll'd to larboard, when the surge was
    seething free,
Where the wallowing monster spouted his foam-fountains in
    the sea.
Let us swear an oath, and keep it with an equal mind,
In the hollow Lotos-land to live and lie reclined
On the hills like Gods together, careless of mankind.
For they lie beside their nectar, and the bolts are hurl'd
Far below them in the valleys, and the clouds are lightly
    curl'd
Round their golden houses, girdled with the gleaming world ;
Where they smile in secret, looking over wasted lands,
Blight and famine, plague and earthquake, roaring deeps
    and fiery sands,   160
Clanging fights, and flaming towns, and sinking ships, and
    praying hands.
But they smile, they find a music centred in a doleful song
Steaming up, a lamentation and an ancient tale of wrong,
Like a tale of little meaning tho' the words are strong ;
Chanted from an ill-used race of men that cleave the soil,
Sow the seed, and reap the harvest with enduring toil,
Storing yearly little dues of wheat and wine and oil ;

Till they perish and they suffer — some, 't is whisper'd —
    down in hell
Suffer endless anguish, others in Elysian valleys dwell,
Resting weary limbs at last on beds of asphodel.   170
Surely, surely, slumber is more sweet than toil, the shore
Than labor in the deep mid-ocean, wind and wave and oar ;
O rest ye, brother mariners, we will not wander more.

THE PALACE OF ART.

I BUILT my soul a lordly pleasure-house,
    Wherein at ease for aye to dwell.
I said, ' O Soul, make merry and carouse,
    Dear soul, for all is well.'

A huge crag-platform, smooth as burnish'd brass,
    I chose.   The ranged ramparts bright
From level meadow-bases of deep grass
    Suddenly scaled the light.

Thereon I built it firm.   Of ledge or shelf
    The rock rose clear, or winding stair.   10
My soul would live alone unto herself
    In her high palace there.

And ' while the world runs round and round,' I said,
    ' Reign thou apart, a quiet king,
Still as, while Saturn whirls, his steadfast shade
    Sleeps on his luminous ring.'

To which my soul made answer readily :
    ' Trust me, in bliss I shall abide
In this great mansion that is built for me,
    So royal-rich and wide.'   20

Four courts I made, East, West, and South, and North,
    In each a squared lawn, wherefrom
The golden gorge of dragons spouted forth
        A flood of fountain-foam.

And round the cool green courts there ran a row
    Of cloisters, branch'd like mighty woods,
Echoing all night to that sonorous flow
        Of spouted fountain-floods.

And round the roofs a gilded gallery,
    That lent broad verge to distant lands,   30
Far as the wild swan wings, to where the sky
        Dipt down to sea and sands.

From those four jets four currents in one swell
    Across the mountain stream'd below
In misty folds, that floating as they fell
        Lit up a torrent-bow.

And high on every peak a statue seem'd
    To hang on tiptoe, tossing up
A cloud of incense of all odor steam'd
        From out a golden cup.   40

So that she thought, 'And who shall gaze upon
    My palace with unblinded eyes,
While this great bow will waver in the sun,
        And that sweet incense rise?'

For that sweet incense rose and never fail'd,
    And, while day sank or mounted higher,
The light aërial gallery, golden-rail'd,
        Burnt like a fringe of fire.

4

Likewise the deep-set windows, stain'd and traced,
   Would seem slow-flaming crimson fires   50
From shadow'd grots of arches interlaced,
   And tipt with frost-like spires.

.   .   .   .

Full of long-sounding corridors it was,
   That over-vaulted grateful gloom,
Thro' which the livelong day my soul did pass,
   Well-pleased, from room to room.

Full of great rooms and small the palace stood,
   All various, each a perfect whole
From living Nature, fit for every mood
   And change of my still soul.   60

For some were hung with arras green and blue,
   Showing a gaudy summer-morn,
Where with puff'd cheek the belted hunter blew
   His wreathed bugle-horn.

One seem'd all dark and red, — a tract of sand,
   And some one pacing there alone,
Who paced forever in a glimmering land,
   Lit with a low large moon.

One show'd an iron coast and angry waves.
   You seem'd to hear them climb and fall   70
And roar rock-thwarted under bellowing caves,
   Beneath the windy wall.

And one, a full-fed river winding slow
   By herds upon an endless plain,
The ragged rims of thunder brooding low,
   With shadow-streaks of rain.

And one, the reapers at their sultry toil.
    In front they bound the sheaves.   Behind
Were realms of upland, prodigal in oil
    And hoary to the wind.   80

And one, a foreground black with stones and slags,
    Beyond, a line of heights, and higher
All barr'd with long white cloud the scornful crags,
    And highest, snow and fire.

And one, an English home, — gray twilight pour'd
    On dewy pastures, dewy trees,
Softer than sleep, — all things in order stored,
    A haunt of ancient Peace.

Nor these alone, but every landscape fair,
    As fit for every mood of mind,   90
Or gay, or grave, or sweet, or stern, was there,
    Not less than truth design'd.

    .   .   .   .

Or the maid-mother by a crucifix,
    In tracts of pasture sunny-warm,
Beneath branch-work of costly sardonyx
    Sat smiling, babe in arm.

Or in a clear-wall'd city on the sea,
    Near gilded organ-pipes, her hair
Wound with white roses, slept Saint Cecily;
    An angel look'd at her.   100

Or thronging all one porch of Paradise,
    A group of Houris bow'd to see
The dying Islamite, with hands and eyes
    That said, We wait for thee.

Or mythic Uther's deeply-wounded son
   In some fair space of sloping greens
Lay, dozing in the vale of Avalon,
     And watch'd by weeping queens.

Or hollowing one hand against his ear,
   To list a footfall, ere he saw
The wood-nymph, stay'd the Ausonian king to hear
     Of wisdom and of law.

Or over hills with peaky tops engrail'd,
   And many a tract of palm and rice,
The throne of Indian Cama slowly sail'd
   A summer fann'd with spice.

Or sweet Europa's mantle blew unclasp'd,
   From off her shoulder backward borne :
From one hand droop'd a crocus ; one hand grasp'd
   The mild bull's golden horn.   120

Or else flush'd Ganymede, his rosy thigh
   Half-buried in the eagle's down,
Sole as a flying star shot thro' the sky
   Above the pillar'd town.

Nor these alone ; but every legend fair
   Which the supreme Caucasian mind
Carved out of Nature for itself, was there,
   Not less than life design'd.

   .   .   .   .

Then in the towers I placed great bells that swung,
   Moved of themselves, with silver sound ;   130
And with choice paintings of wise men I hung
   The royal dais round.

For there was Milton like a seraph strong,
   Beside him Shakespeare bland and mild ;
And there the world-worn Dante grasp'd his song,
   And somewhat grimly smiled.

And there the Ionian father of the rest ;
   A million wrinkles carved his skin ;
A hundred winters snow'd upon his breast,
   From cheek and throat and chin.   140

Above, the fair hall-ceiling stately-set
  Many an arch high up did lift,
And angels rising and descending met
  With interchange of gift.

Below was all mosaic choicely plann'd
  With cycles of the human tale
Of this wide world, the times of every land
  So wrought, they will not fail.

The people here, a beast of burden slow,
  Toil'd onward, prick'd with goads and stings ;   150
Here play'd a tiger, rolling to and fro
  The heads and crowns of kings ;

Here rose an athlete, strong to break or bind
  All force in bonds that might endure,
And here once more like some sick man declin'd,
  And trusted any cure.

But over these she trod ; and those great bells
  Began to chime. She took her throne ;
She sat betwixt the shining oriels,
  To sing her songs alone.   160

And thro' the topmost oriels' color'd flame
  Two godlike faces gazed below ;
Plato the wise, and large-brow'd Verulam,
  The first of those who know.

And all those names, that in their motion were
  Full-welling fountain-heads of change,
Betwixt the slender shafts were blazon'd fair
  In diverse raiment strange ;

Thro' which the lights, rose, amber, emerald, blue,
   Flush'd in her temples and her eyes,   170
And from her lips, as morn from Memnon, drew
   Rivers of melodies.

No nightingale delighteth to prolong
   Her low preamble all alone,
More than my soul to hear her echo'd song
   Throb thro' the ribbed stone ;

Singing and murmuring in her feastful mirth,
   Joying to feel herself alive,
Lord over Nature, lord of the visible earth,
   Lord of the senses five ;   180

Communing with herself: ' All these are mine,
   And let the world have peace or wars,
'T is one to me.'   She — when young night divine
   Crown'd dying day with stars,

Making sweet close of his delicious toils —
   Lit light in wreaths and anadems,
And pure quintessences of precious oils
   In hollow'd moons of gems,

To mimic heaven ; and clapt her hands and cried,
   ' I marvel if my still delight   190
In this great house so royal-rich and wide
   Be flatter'd to the height.

' O all things fair to sate my various eyes !
   O shapes and hues that please me well !
O silent faces of the Great and Wise,
   My Gods, with whom I dwell !

'O Godlike isolation which art mine,
   I can but count thee perfect gain,
What time I watch the darkening droves of swine
    That range on yonder plain.

'In filthy sloughs they roll a prurient skin,
   They graze and wallow, breed and sleep ;
And oft some brainless devil enters in,
    And drives them to the deep.'

.

Then of the moral instinct would she prate,
   And of the rising from the dead,
As hers by right of full-accomplish'd Fate ;
    And at the last she said :

'I take possession of man's mind and deed.
   I care not what the sects may brawl.
I sit as God holding no form of creed,
    But contemplating all.'

.   .   .   .   .   .

Full oft the riddle of the painful earth
   Flash'd thro' her as she sat alone,
Yet not the less held she her solemn mirth,
    And intellectual throne.

.

And so she throve and prosper'd ; so three years
   She prosper'd : on the fourth she fell,
Like Herod, when the shout was in his ears,
    Struck thro' with pangs of hell.

Lest she should fail and perish utterly,
   God, before whom ever lie bare
The abysmal deeps of personality,
    Plagued her with sore despair.

When she would think, where'er she turn'd her sight
   The airy hand confusion wrought,
Wrote 'Mene, mene,' and divided quite
   The kingdom of her thought.

Deep dread and loathing of her solitude
   Fell on her, from which mood was born   230
Scorn of herself; again, from out that mood
   Laughter at her self-scorn.

'What! is not this my place of strength,' she said,
   'My spacious mansion built for me,
Whereof the strong foundation-stones were laid
   Since my first memory?'

But in dark corners of her palace stood
   Uncertain shapes; and unawares
On white-eyed phantasms weeping tears of blood,
   And horrible nightmares,   240

And hollow shades enclosing hearts of flame,
   And, with dim fretted foreheads all,
On corpses three-months-old at noon she came,
   That stood against the wall.

A spot of dull stagnation, without light
   Or power of movement, seem'd my soul,
'Mid onward-sloping motions infinite
   Making for one sure goal.

A still salt pool, lock'd in with bars of sand,
   Left on the shore; that hears all night   250
The plunging seas draw backward from the land
   Their moon-led waters white.

A star that with the choral starry dance
    Join'd not, but stood, and standing saw
The hollow orb of moving Circumstance
    Roll'd round by one fixt law.

Back on herself her serpent pride had curl'd.
    ' No voice,' she shriek'd in that lone hall,
' No voice breaks thro' the stillness of this world !
    One deep, deep silence all ! '

She, mouldering with the dull earth's mouldering sod,
    Inwrapt tenfold in slothful shame,
Lay there exiled from eternal God,
    Lost to her place and name ;

And death and life she hated equally,
    And nothing saw, for her despair,
But dreadful time, dreadful eternity,
    No comfort anywhere ;

Remaining utterly confused with fears,
    And ever worse with growing time,
And ever unrelieved by dismal tears,
    And all alone in crime.

Shut up as in a crumbling tomb, girt round
    With blackness as a solid wall,
Far off she seem'd to hear the dully sound
    Of human footsteps fall :

As in strange lands a traveller walking slow,
    In doubt and great perplexity,
A little before moon-rise hears the low
    Moan of an unknown sea ;

And knows not if it be thunder or a sound
  Of rocks thrown down, or one deep cry
Of great wild beasts ; then thinketh, ' I have found
  A new land, but I die.'

She howl'd aloud, ' I am on fire within.
  There comes no murmur of reply.
What is it that will take away my sin,
  And save me lest I die ? '

So when four years were wholly finished,
  She threw her royal robes away.   290
' Make me a cottage in the vale,' she said,
  ' Where I may mourn and pray.

' Yet pull not down my palace towers, that are
  So lightly, beautifully built ;
Perchance I may return with others there
  When I have purged my guilt.'

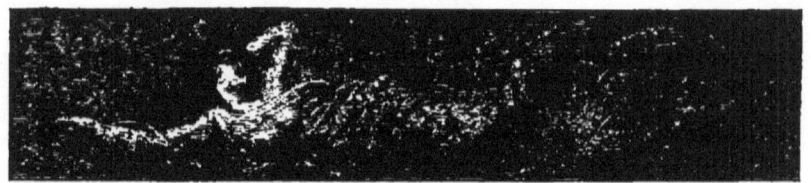

A DREAM OF FAIR WOMEN.

I READ, before my eyelids dropt their shade,
    ' *The Legend of Good Women*,' long ago
Sung by the morning star of song, who made
    His music heard below ;

Dan Chaucer, the first warbler, whose sweet breath
    Preluded those melodious bursts that fill
The spacious times of great Elizabeth
    With sounds that echo still.

And, for a while, the knowledge of his art
    Held me above the subject, as strong gales   10
Hold swollen clouds from raining, tho' my heart,
    Brimful of those wild tales,

Charged both mine eyes with tears.   In every land
    I saw, wherever light illumineth,
Beauty and anguish walking hand in hand
    The downward slope to death.

Those far-renowned brides of ancient song
    Peopled the hollow dark, like burning stars,
And I heard sounds of insult, shame, and wrong,
    And trumpets blown for wars ;   20

And clattering flints batter'd with clanging hoofs :
    And I saw crowds in column'd sanctuaries ;
And forms that past at windows and on roofs
    Of marble palaces ;

Corpses across the threshold ; heroes tall
    Dislodging pinnacle and parapet
Upon the tortoise creeping to the wall ;
    Lances in ambush set ;

And high shrine-doors burst thro' with heated blasts
    That run before the fluttering tongues of fire ;   30
White surf wind-scatter'd over sails and masts,
    And ever climbing higher ;

Squadrons and squares of men in brazen plates,
    Scaffolds, still sheets of water, divers woes,
Ranges of glimmering vaults with iron grates,
    And hush'd seraglios.

So shape chased shape as swift as, when to land
    Bluster the winds and tides the selfsame way,
Crisp foam-flakes scud along the level sand,
    Torn from the fringe of spray.   40

I started once, or seem'd to start in pain,
    Resolved on noble things, and strove to speak,
As when a great thought strikes along the brain,
    And flushes all the cheek.

And once my arm was lifted to hew down
    A cavalier from off his saddle-bow,
That bore a lady from a leaguer'd town ;
    And then, I know not how,

All those sharp fancies by down-lapsing thought
    Stream'd onward, lost their edges, and did creep   50
Roll'd on each other, rounded, smooth'd, and brought
    Into the gulfs of sleep.

At last methought that I had wandered far
    In an old wood : fresh-wash'd in coolest dew,
The maiden splendors of the morning star
    Shook in the steadfast blue.

Enormous elm-tree boles did stoop and lean
    Upon the dusky brushwood underneath
Their broad curved branches, fledged with clearest green,
    New from its silken sheath.   ·   60

The dim red morn had died, her journey done,
    And with dead lips smiled at the twilight plain,
Half-fallen across the threshold of the sun,
    Never to rise again.

There was no motion in the dumb dead air,
    Not any song of bird or sound of rill ;
Gross darkness of the inner sepulchre
    Is not so deadly still

As that wide forest.   Growths of jasmine turn'd
    Their humid arms festooning tree to tree,   70
And at the root thro' lush green grasses burn'd
    The red anemone.

I knew the flowers, I knew the leaves, I knew
    The tearful glimmer of the languid dawn
On those long, rank, dark wood-walks drench'd in dew,
    Leading from lawn to lawn.

The smell of violets, hidden in the green,
    Pour'd back into my empty soul and frame
The times when I remember to have been
    Joyful and free from blame.   80

And from within me a clear undertone
    Thrill'd thro' mine ears in that unblissful clime,
'Pass freely thro'; the wood is all thine own,
    Until the end of time.'

At length I saw a lady within call,
    Stiller than chisell'd marble, standing there;
A daughter of the gods, divinely tall,
    And most divinely fair.

Her loveliness with shame and with surprise
    Froze my swift speech; she turning on my face   90
The star-like sorrows of immortal eyes,
    Spoke slowly in her place.

'I had great beauty; ask thou not my name:
  No one can be more wise than destiny.
Many drew swords and died.   Where'er I came
  I brought calamity.'

'No marvel, sovereign lady: in fair field
  Myself for such a face had boldly died,'
I answer'd free; and turning I appeal'd
  To one that stood beside.   100

But she, with sick and scornful looks averse,
  To her full height her stately stature draws;
'My youth,' she said, 'was blasted with a curse;
  This woman was the cause.

'I was cut off from hope in that sad place
  Which men call'd Aulis in those iron years:
My father held his hand upon his face;
  I, blinded with my tears,

'Still strove to speak: my voice was thick with sighs
  As in a dream.   Dimly I could descry   110
The stern black-bearded kings with wolfish eyes,
  Waiting to see me die.

'The high masts flicker'd as they lay afloat;
  The crowds, the temples, waver'd, and the shore;
The bright death quiver'd at the victim's throat;
  Touch'd; and I knew no more.'

Whereto the other with a downward brow:
  'I would the white cold heavy-plunging foam,
Whirl'd by the wind, had roll'd me deep below,
  Then when I left my home.'   120

Her slow full words sank thro' the silence drear,
    As thunder-drops fall on a sleeping sea :
Sudden I heard a voice that cried, ' Come here,
    That I may look on thee.'

I turning saw, throned on a flowery rise,
    One sitting on a crimson scarf unroll'd ;
A queen, with swarthy cheeks and bold black eyes,
    Brow-bound with burning gold.

She, flashing forth a haughty smile, began :
    ' I govern'd men by change, and so I sway'd   130
All moods. 'T is long since I have seen a man.
    Once, like the moon, I made

' The ever-shifting currents of the blood
    According to my humor ebb and flow.
I have no men to govern in this wood :
    That makes my only woe.

' Nay — yet it chafes me that I could not bend
    One will ; nor tame and tutor with mine eye
That dull cold-blooded Cæsar. Prithee, friend,
    Where is Mark Antony ?   140

' The man, my lover, with whom I rode sublime
    On Fortune's neck : we sat as God by God ;
The Nilus would have risen before his time
    And flooded at our nod.

' We drank the Libyan Sun to sleep, and lit
    Lamps which outburn'd Canopus. O my life
In Egypt ! O the dalliance and the wit,
    The flattery and the strife,

'And the wild kiss, when fresh from war's alarms,
    My Hercules, my Roman Antony,   150
My mailed Bacchus leapt into my arms,
    Contented there to die !

'And there he died ; and when I heard my name
    Sigh'd forth with life I would not brook my fear
Of the other : with a worm I balk'd his fame.
    What else was left? look here !'

(With that she tore her robe apart, and half
    The polish'd argent of her breast to sight
Laid bare.   Thereto she pointed with a laugh,
    Showing the aspic's bite.)   160

'I died a queen.   The Roman soldier found
    Me lying dead, my crown about my brows,
A name forever ! — lying robed and crown'd,
    Worthy a Roman spouse.'

Her warbling voice, a lyre of widest range
    Struck by all passion, did fall down and glance
From tone to tone, and glided thro' all change
    Of liveliest utterance.

When she made pause I knew not for delight ;
    Because with sudden motion from the ground   170
She raised her piercing orbs, and fill'd with light
    The interval of sound.

Still with their fires Love tipt his keenest darts ;
    As once they drew into two burning rings
All beams of Love, melting the mighty hearts
    Of captains and of kings.

Slowly my sense undazzled.   Then I heard
    A noise of some one coming thro' the lawn,
And singing clearer than the crested bird
    That claps his wings at dawn.   180

'The torrent brooks of hallow'd Israel
    From craggy hollows pouring, late and soon,
Sound all night long, in falling thro' the dell,
    Far-heard beneath the moon.

'The balmy moon of blessed Israel
    Floods all the deep-blue gloom with beams divine ;
All night the splinter'd crags that wall the dell
    With spires of silver shine.'

As one that museth where broad sunshine laves
    The lawn of some cathedral, thro' the door   190
Hearing the holy organ rolling waves
    Of sound on roof and floor

Within, and anthem sung, is charm'd and tied
    To where he stands, — so stood I, when that flow
Of music left the lips of her that died
    To save her father's vow ;

The daughter of the warrior Gileadite,
    A maiden pure ; as when she went along
From Mizpeh's tower'd gate with welcome light,
    With timbrel and with song.   200

My words leapt forth : 'Heaven heads the count of crimes
    With that wild oath.'   She render'd answer high :
'Not so, nor once alone ; a thousand times
    I would be born and die.

'Single I grew, like some green plant, whose root
    Creeps to the garden water-pipes beneath,
Feeding the flower ; but ere my flower to fruit
    Changed, I was ripe for death.

'My God, my land, my father, — these did move
    Me from my bliss of life, that Nature gave,   210
Lower'd softly with a threefold cord of love
    Down to a silent grave.

'And I went mourning, "No fair Hebrew boy
    Shall smile away my maiden blame among
The Hebrew mothers " — emptied of all joy,
    Leaving the dance and song,

'Leaving the olive-gardens far below,
    Leaving the promise of my bridal bower,
The valleys of grape-loaded vines that glow
    Beneath the battled tower.   220

'The light white cloud swam over us.   Anon
    We heard the lion roaring from his den ;
We saw the large white stars rise one by one,
    Or, from the darken'd glen,

'Saw God divide the night with flying flame,
    And thunder on the everlasting hills.
I heard Him, for He spake, and grief became
    A solemn scorn of ills.

'When the next moon was roll'd into the sky,
    Strength came to me that equall'd my desire.   230
How beautiful a thing it was to die
    For God and for my sire !

'It comforts me in this one thought to dwell,
    That I subdued me to my father's will;
Because the kiss he gave me, ere I fell,
    Sweetens the spirit still.

'Moreover it is written that my race
    Hew'd Ammon, hip and thigh, from Aroer
On Arnon unto Minneth.'   Here her face
    Glow'd, as I look'd at her.   240

She lock'd her lips; she left me where I stood: ·
    'Glory to God,' she sang, and past afar,
Thridding the sombre boscage of the wood,
    Toward the morning-star.

Losing her carol I stood pensively,
    As one that from a casement leans his head,
When midnight bells cease ringing suddenly,
    And the old year is dead.

'Alas! alas!' a low voice, full of care,
    Murmur'd beside me: 'Turn and look on me;   250
I am that Rosamond, whom men call fair,
    If what I was I be.

'Would I had been some maiden coarse and poor!
    O me, that I should ever see the light!
Those dragon eyes of anger'd Eleanor
    Do hunt me, day and night.'

She ceased in tears, fallen from hope and trust:
    To whom the Egyptian: 'O, you tamely died!
You should have clung to Fulvia's waist, and thrust
    The dagger thro' her side.'   260

With that sharp sound the white dawn's creeping beams,
    Stolen to my brain, dissolved the mystery
Of folded sleep.   The captain of my dreams
    Ruled in the eastern sky.

Morn broaden'd on the borders of the dark,
    Ere I saw her who clasp'd in her last trance
Her murder'd father's head, or Joan of Arc,
    A light of ancient France ;

Or her who knew that Love can vanquish Death,
    Who kneeling, with one arm about her king,   270
Drew forth the poison with her balmy breath,
    Sweet as new buds in Spring.

No memory labors longer from the deep
    Gold-mines of thought to lift the hidden ore
That glimpses, moving up, than I from sleep
    To gather and tell o'er

Each little sound and sight.   With what dull pain
    Compass'd, how eagerly I sought to strike
Into that wondrous track of dreams again !
    But no two dreams are like.   280

As when a soul laments, which hath been blest,
    Desiring what is mingled with past years,
In yearnings that can never be exprest
    By signs or groans or tears ;

Because all words, tho' cull'd with choicest art,
    Failing to give the bitter of the sweet,
Wither beneath the palate, and the heart
    Faints, faded by its heat.

THE EPIC.

AT Francis Allen's on the Christmas-eve, —
The game of forfeits done — the girls all kiss'd
Beneath the sacred bush and past away —
The parson Holmes, the poet Everard Hall,
The host, and I sat round the wassail-bowl,

Then half-way ebb'd : and there we held a talk,
How all the old honor had from Christmas gone,
Or gone or dwindled down to some odd games
In some odd nooks like this ; till I, tired out
With cutting eights that day upon the pond,
Where, three times slipping from the outer edge,
I bump'd the ice into three several stars,
Fell in a doze ; and half-awake I heard
The parson taking wide and wider sweeps,
Now harping on the church-commissioners,
Now hawking at geology and schism ;
Until I woke, and found him settled down
Upon the general decay of faith
Right thro' the world, 'at home was little left,
And none abroad : there was no anchor, none,
To hold by.'   Francis, laughing, clapt his hand
On Everard's shoulder, with 'I hold by him.'
'And I,' quoth Everard, 'by the wassail-bowl.'
'Why yes,' I said, 'we knew your gift that way
At college ; but another which you had —
I mean of verse (for so we held it then),
What came of that?'   'You know,' said Frank, 'he burnt
His epic, his King Arthur, some twelve books ' —
And then to me demanding why?   ' O, sir,
He thought that nothing new was said, or else
Something so said 't was nothing — that a truth
Looks freshest in the fashion of the day :
God knows : he has a mint of reasons : ask.
It pleased *me* well enough.'   'Nay, nay,' said Hall,
'Why take the style of those heroic times?
For nature brings not back the mastodon,
Nor we those times ; and why should any man
Remodel models? these twelve books of mine
Were faint Homeric echoes, nothing-worth,
Mere chaff and draff, much better burnt.'   'But I,'

Said Francis, ' pick'd the eleventh from this hearth,
And have it : keep a thing, its use will come.
I hoard it as a sugar-plum for Holmes.'
He laugh'd, and I, tho' sleepy, like a horse
That hears the corn-bin open, prick'd my ears ;
For I remember'd Everard's college fame
When we were Freshmen : then at my request
He brought it ; and the poet, little urged,
But with some prelude of disparagement,
Read, mouthing out his hollow oes and aes,   50
Deep-chested music, and to this result.

MORTE D'ARTHUR.

So all day long the noise of battle roll'd
Among the mountains by the winter sea ;
Until King Arthur's table, man by man,
Had fallen in Lyonness about their lord,
King Arthur : then, because his wound was deep,
The bold Sir Bedivere uplifted him,
Sir Bedivere, the last of all his knights,
And bore him to a chapel nigh the field,
A broken chancel with a broken cross,   60
That stood on a dark strait of barren land.
On one side lay the ocean, and on one
Lay a great water, and the moon was full.
    Then spake King Arthur to Sir Bedivere :
' The sequel of to-day unsolders all
The goodliest fellowship of famous knights
Whereof this world holds record.   Such a sleep
They sleep — the men I loved.   I think that we
Shall never more, at any future time,
Delight our souls with talk of knightly deeds,   70
Walking about the gardens and the halls

Of Camelot, as in the days that were.
I perish by this people which I made, —
Tho' Merlin sware that I should come again
To rule once more — but let what will be, be,
I am so deeply smitten thro' the helm
That without help I cannot last till morn.
Thou therefore take my brand Excalibur,
Which was my pride : for thou rememberest how
In those old days, one summer noon, an arm   80
Rose up from out the bosom of the lake,
Clothed in white samite, mystic, wonderful,
Holding the sword — and how I row'd across
And took it, and have worn it, like a king ;
And, wheresoever I am sung or told
In aftertime, this also shall be known :
But now delay not ; take Excalibur,
And fling him far into the middle mere ;
Watch what thou seest, and lightly bring me word.'
    To him replied the bold Sir Bedivere :   90
'It is not meet, Sir King, to leave thee thus,
Aidless, alone, and smitten thro' the helm.
A little thing may harm a wounded man.
Yet I thy hest will all perform at full,
Watch what I see, and lightly bring thee word.'
    So saying, from the ruin'd shrine he stept
And in the moon athwart the place of tombs,
Where lay the mighty bones of ancient men,
Old knights, and over them the sea-wind sang
Shrill, chill, with flakes of foam.   He, stepping down   100
By zigzag paths and juts of pointed rock,
Came on the shining levels of the lake.
    There drew he forth the brand Excalibur,
And o'er him, drawing it, the winter moon,
Brightening the skirts of a long cloud, ran forth
And sparkled keen with frost against the hilt :

For all the haft twinkled with diamond studs,
Myriads of topaz-lights, and jacinth-work
Of subtlest jewellery.   He gazed so long
That both his eyes were dazzled, as he stood,   110
This way and that dividing the swift mind,
In act to throw; but at the last it seem'd
Better to leave Excalibur conceal'd
There in the many-knotted water-flags,
That whistled stiff and dry about the marge.
So strode he back slow to the wounded king.
    Then spake King Arthur to Sir Bedivere :
' Hast thou perform'd my mission which I gave?
What is it thou hast seen, or what hast heard?'
    And answer made the bold Sir Bedivere :   120
' I heard the ripple washing in the reeds,
And the wild water lapping on the crag.'
    To whom replied King Arthur, faint and pale :
'Thou hast betray'd thy nature and thy name,
Not rendering true answer, as beseem'd
Thy fealty, nor like a noble knight ;
For surer sign had follow'd, either hand,
Or voice, or else a motion of the mere.
This is a shameful thing for men to lie.
Yet now, I charge thee, quickly go again   130
As thou art lief and dear, and do the thing
I bade thee, watch, and lightly bring me word.'
    Then went Sir Bedivere the second time
Across the ridge, and paced beside the mere,
Counting the dewy pebbles, fix'd in thought ;
But when he saw the wonder of the hilt,
How curiously and strangely chased, he smote
His palms together, and he cried aloud.
    ' And if indeed I cast the brand away,
Surely a precious thing, one worthy note,   140
Should thus be lost forever from the earth,

Which might have pleased the eyes of many men.
What good should follow this, if this were done?
What harm, undone? deep harm to disobey,
Seeing obedience is the bond of rule.
Were it well to obey then, if a king demand
An act unprofitable, against himself?
The king is sick, and knows not what he does.
What record, or what relic of my lord
Should be to aftertime, but empty breath   150
And rumors of a doubt? but were this kept,
Stored in some treasure-house of mighty kings,
Some one might show it at a joust of arms,
Saying, " King Arthur's sword, Excalibur,
Wrought by the lonely maiden of the lake.
Nine years she wrought it, sitting in the deeps
Upon the hidden bases of the hills."
So might some old man speak in the aftertime
To all the people, winning reverence ;
But now much honor and much fame were lost.'   160
    So spake he, clouded with his own conceit,
And hid Excalibur the second time,
And so strode back slow to the wounded king.
    Then spoke King Arthur, breathing heavily :
' What is it thou hast seen, or what hast heard?'
    And answer made the bold Sir Bedivere :
' I heard the water lapping on the crag,
And the long ripple washing in the reeds.'
    To whom replied King Arthur, much in wrath :
' Ah, miserable and unkind, untrue,   170
Unknightly, traitor-hearted !   Woe is me !
Authority forgets a dying king,
Laid widow'd of the power in his eye
That bow'd the will.   I see thee what thou art,
For thou, the latest-left of all my knights,
In whom should meet the offices of all,

Thou wouldst betray me for the precious hilt ;
Either from lust of gold, or like a girl
Valuing the giddy pleasure of the eyes.
Yet, for a man may fail in duty twice,   180
And the third time may prosper, get thee hence ;
But, if thou spare to fling Excalibur,
I will arise and slay thee with my hands.'
    Then quickly rose Sir Bedivere, and ran,
And, leaping down the ridges lightly, plunged
Among the bulrush-beds, and clutch'd the sword,
And strongly wheel'd and threw it.   The great brand
Made lightnings in the splendor of the moon,
And flashing round and round, and whirl'd in an arch,
Shot like a streamer of the northern morn,   190
Seen where the moving isles of winter shock
By night, with noises of the northern sea.
So flash'd and fell the brand Excalibur :
But ere he dipt the surface, rose an arm
Cloth'd in white samite, mystic, wonderful,
And caught him by the hilt, and brandish'd him
Three times, and drew him under in the mere.
And lightly went the other to the king.
    Then spoke King Arthur, drawing thicker breath :
' Now see I by thine eyes that this is done.   200
Speak out : what is it thou hast heard, or seen ? '
    And answer made the bold Sir Bedivere :
' Sir King, I closed mine eyelids, lest the gems
Should blind my purpose, for I never saw,
Nor shall see, here or elsewhere, till I die,
Not tho' I live three lives of mortal men,
So great a miracle as yonder hilt.
Then with both hands I flung him, wheeling him ;
But when I look'd again, behold an arm,
Clothed in white samite, mystic, wonderful,   210
That caught him by the hilt, and brandish'd him
Three times, and drew him under in the mere.'

And answer made King Arthur, breathing hard :
' My end draws nigh ; 't is time that I were gone.
Make broad thy shoulders to receive my weight,
And bear me to the margin ; yet I fear
My wound hath taken cold, and I shall die.'
 So saying, from the pavement he half rose,
Slowly, with pain, reclining on his arm,
And looking wistfully with wide blue eyes   220
As in a picture. Him Sir Bedivere
Remorsefully regarded thro' his tears,
And would have spoken, but he found not words, .
Then took with care, and kneeling on one knee,
O'er both his shoulders drew the languid hands,
And rising bore him thro' the place of tombs.
 But, as he walk'd, King Arthur panted hard,
Like one that feels a nightmare on his bed
When all the house is mute. So sigh'd the king,
Muttering and murmuring at his ear, ' Quick, quick ! 230
I fear it is too late, and I shall die.'
But the other swiftly strode from ridge to ridge,
Clothed with his breath, and looking, as he walk'd,
Larger than human on the frozen hills.
He heard the deep behind him, and a cry
Before. His own thought drove him like a goad.
Dry clash'd his harness in the icy caves
And barren chasms, and all to left and right
The bare black cliff clang'd round him, as he based
His feet on juts of slippery crag that rang 240
Sharp-smitten with the dint of armed heels —
And on a sudden, lo ! the level lake,
And the long glories of the winter moon.
 Then saw they how there hove a dusky barge,
Dark as a funeral scarf from stem to stern,
Beneath them ; and descending they were ware
That all the decks were dense with stately forms
Black-stoled, black-hooded, like a dream — by these

Three queens with crowns of gold — and from them rose
A cry that shiver'd to the tingling stars,   250
And, as it were one voice, an agony
Of lamentation, like a wind, that shrills
All night in a waste land, where no one comes,
Or hath come, since the making of the world.
     Then murmur'd Arthur, ' Place me in the barge,'
And to the barge they came.   There those three queens
Put forth their hands, and took the king, and wept.
But she that rose the tallest of them all
And fairest, laid his head upon her lap,
And loosed the shatter'd casque, and chafed his hands,   260
And call'd him by his name, complaining loud,
And dropping bitter tears against his brow
Striped with dark blood : for all his face was white
And colorless, and like the wither'd moon
Smote by the fresh beam of the springing east ;
And all his greaves and cuisses dash'd with drops
Of onset ; and the light and lustrous curls —
That made his forehead like a rising sun
High from the dais-throne — were parch'd with dust ;
Or, clotted into points and hanging loose,   270
Mix'd with the knightly growth that fringed his lips.
So like a shatter'd column lay the king ;
Not like that Arthur who, with lance in rest,
From spur to plume a star of tournament,
Shot thro' the lists at Camelot, and charged
Before the eyes of ladies and of kings.
     Then loudly cried the bold Sir Bedivere,
' Ah ! my Lord Arthur, whither shall I go ?
Where shall I hide my forehead and my eyes ?
For now I see the true old times are dead,   280
When every morning brought a noble chance,
And every chance brought out a noble knight.
Such times have been not since the light that led
The holy Elders with the gift of myrrh.

But now the whole ROUND TABLE is dissolved
Which was an image of the mighty world ;
And I, the last, go forth companionless,
And the days darken round me, and the years,
Among new men, strange faces, other minds.'

    And slowly answer'd Arthur from the barge ;   290
' The old order changeth, yielding place to new,
And God fulfils himself in many ways,
Lest one good custom should corrupt the world.
Comfort thyself : what comfort is in me ?
I have lived my life, and that which I have done
May He within himself make pure ! but thou,
If thou shouldst never see my face again,
Pray for my soul.   More things are wrought by prayer
Than this world dreams of.   Wherefore, let thy voice
Rise like a fountain for me night and day.   300
For what are men better than sheep or goats
That nourish a blind life within the brain,
If, knowing God, they lift not hands of prayer
Both for themselves and those who call them friend ?
For so the whole round earth is every way
Bound by gold chains about the feet of God.
But now farewell.   I am going a long way
With these thou seest — if indeed I go —
(For all my mind is clouded with a doubt)
To the island-valley of Avilion ;   310
Where falls not hail, or rain, or any snow,
Nor ever wind blows loudly ; but it lies
Deep-meadow'd, happy, fair with orchard lawns
And bowery hollows crown'd with summer sea,
Where I will heal me of my grievous wound.'

    So said he, and the barge with oar and sail
Moved from the brink, like some full-breasted swan
That, fluting a wild carol ere her death,
Ruffles her pure cold plume, and takes the flood
With swarthy webs.   Long stood Sir Bedivere   320

Revolving many memories, till the hull
Look'd one black dot against the verge of dawn,
And on the mere the wailing died away.

Here ended Hall, and our last light, that long
Had wink'd and threaten'd darkness, flared and fell;
At which the parson, sent to sleep with sound,
And waked with silence, grunted 'Good!' but we
Sat rapt: it was the tone with which he read —
Perhaps some modern touches here and there
Redeem'd it from the charge of nothingness —   330
Or else we loved the man, and prized his work;
I know not: but we sitting, as I said,
The cock crew loud; as at that time of year
The lusty bird takes every hour for dawn:
Then Francis, muttering, like a man ill-used,
'There now — that's nothing!' drew a little back,
And drove his heel into the smoulder'd log,
That sent a blast of sparkles up the flue:
And so to bed; where yet in sleep I seem'd
To sail with Arthur under looming shores,   340
Point after point; till on to dawn, when dreams
Begin to feel the truth and stir of day,
To me, methought, who waited with the crowd,
There came a bark that, blowing forward, bore
King Arthur, like a modern gentleman
Of stateliest port; and all the people cried,
'Arthur is come again: he cannot die.'
Then those that stood upon the hills behind
Repeated — 'Come again, and thrice as fair;'
And, further inland, voices echoed — 'Come   350
With all good things, and war shall be no more.'
At this a hundred bells began to peal,
That with the sound I woke, and heard indeed
The clear church-bells ring in the Christmas morn.

6

THE TALKING OAK.

ONCE more the gate behind me falls ;
  Once more before my face
I see the moulder'd Abbey-walls,
  That stand within the chace.

Beyond the lodge the city lies,
  Beneath its drift of smoke ;
And ah ! with what delighted eyes
  I turn to yonder oak.

For when my passion first began,
  Ere that which in me burn'd,   10
The love that makes me thrice a man,
  Could hope itself return'd,

To yonder oak within the field
  I spoke without restraint,
And with a larger faith appeal'd
  Than Papist unto Saint.

For oft I talk'd with him apart,
  And told him of my choice,
Until he plagiarized a heart,
  And answer'd with a voice.   20

Tho' what he whisper'd under heaven
  None else could understand,
I found him garrulously given,
  A babbler in the land.

But since I heard him make reply
  Is many a weary hour ;
'T were well to question him, and try
  If yet he keeps the power.

Hail, hidden to the knees in fern,
  Broad Oak of Sumner-chace,   30
Whose topmost branches can discern
  The roofs of Sumner-place !

Say thou, whereon I carved her name,
    If ever maid or spouse,
As fair as my Olivia, came
    To rest beneath thy boughs. —

'O Walter, I have shelter'd here
    Whatever maiden grace
The good old summers, year by year,
    Made ripe in Sumner-chace :

'Old summers, when the monk was fat,
    And, issuing shorn and sleek,
Would twist his girdle tight, and pat
    The girls upon the cheek,

'Ere yet, in scorn of Peter's-pence,
    And number'd bead and shrift,
Bluff Harry broke into the spence,
    And turn'd the cowls adrift :

'And I have seen some score of those
    Fresh faces that would thrive
When his man-minded offset rose
    To chase the deer at five ;

'And all that from the town would stroll,
    Till that wild wind made work
In which the gloomy brewer's soul
    Went by me, like a stork :

'The slight she-slips of loyal blood,
    And others, passing praise,
Strait-laced, but all-too-full in bud
    For puritanic stays :

'And I have shadow'd many a group
    Of beauties that were born
In teacup-times of hood and hoop,
    Or while the patch was worn ;

'And, leg and arm with love-knots gay,
    About me leap'd and laugh'd
The modish Cupid of the day,
    And shrill'd his tinsel shaft.

'I swear (and else may insects prick
    Each leaf into a gall !)   70
This girl, for whom your heart is sick,
    Is three times worth them all ;

'For those and theirs, by Nature's law,
    Have faded long ago ;
But in these latter springs I saw
    Your own Olivia blow,

'From when she gamboll'd on the greens,
    A baby-germ, to when
The maiden blossoms of her teens
    Could number five from ten.   80

'I swear, by leaf, and wind, and rain
    (And hear me with thine ears),
That, tho' I circle in the grain
    Five hundred rings of years —

'Yet, since I first could cast a shade,
    Did never creature pass
So slightly, musically made,
    So light upon the grass :

'For as to fairies, that will flit
    To make the greensward fresh,
I hold them exquisitely knit,
    But far too spare of flesh.'

O, hide thy knotted knees in fern,
    And overlook the chace;
And from thy topmost branch discern
    The roofs of Sumner-place.

But thou, whereon I carved her name,
    That oft hast heard my vows,
Declare when last Olivia came
    To sport beneath thy boughs.

'O yesterday, you know, the fair
    Was holden at the town;
Her father left his good arm-chair,
    And rode his hunter down.

'And with him Albert came on his,
    I look'd at him with joy;
As cowslip unto oxlip is,
    So seems she to the boy.

'An hour had past — and, sitting straight
    Within the low-wheel'd chaise,
Her mother trundled to the gate
    Behind the dappled grays.

'But, as for her, she stay'd at home,
    And on the roof she went,
And down the way you use to come
    She look'd with discontent.

'She left the novel half-uncut
　　Upon the rosewood shelf;
She left the new piano shut:
　　She could not please herself.　　　120

'Then ran she, gamesome as the colt,
　　And livelier than a lark
She sent her voice thro' all the holt
　　Before her, and the park.

'A light wind chased her on the wing,
　　And in the chase grew wild;
As close as might be would he cling
　　About the darling child:

'But light as any wind that blows
　　So fleetly did she stir,　　　130
The flower she touch'd on dipt and rose,
　　And turn'd to look at her.

'And here she came, and round me play'd,
　　And sang to me the whole
Of those three stanzas that you made
　　About my " giant bole ; "

'And in a fit of frolic mirth
　　She strove to span my waist;
Alas, I was so broad of girth,
　　I could not be embraced !　　　140

'I wish'd myself the fair young beech
　　That here beside me stands,
That round me, clasping each in each,
　　She might have lock'd her hands.

'Yet seem'd the pressure thrice as sweet
    As woodbine's fragile hold,
Or when I feel about my feet
    The berried briony fold.'

O muffle round thy knees with fern,
    And shadow Sumner-chace !
Long may thy topmost branch discern
    The roofs of Sumner-place !

But tell me, did she read the name
    I carved with many vows
When last with throbbing heart I came
    To rest beneath thy boughs?

'O yes, she wander'd round and round
    These knotted knees of mine,
And found, and kiss'd the name she found,
    And sweetly murmur'd thine.

'A teardrop trembled from its source,
    And down my surface crept.
My sense of touch is something coarse,
    But I believe she wept.

'Then flush'd her cheek with rosy light,
    She glanced across the plain ;
But not a creature was in sight ;
    She kiss'd me once again.

'Her kisses were so close and kind,
    That, trust me on my word,
Hard wood I am, and wrinkled rind,
    But yet my sap was stirr'd ;

'And even into my inmost ring
 A pleasure I discern'd,
Like those blind motions of the Spring
 That show the year is turn'd.

'Thrice-happy he that may caress
 The ringlet's waving balm —
The cushions of whose touch may press
 The maiden's tender palm.   180

'I, rooted here among the groves,
 But languidly adjust
My vapid vegetable loves
 With anthers and with dust ;

'For ah ! my friend, the days were brief
 Whereof the poets talk,
When that which breathes within the leaf
 Could slip its bark and walk.

'But could I, as in times foregone,
 From spray and branch and stem,   190
Have suck'd and gather'd into one
 The life that spreads in them,

'She had not found me so remiss ;
 But lightly issuing thro',
I would have paid her kiss for kiss
 With usury thereto.'

O flourish high, with leafy towers,
 And overlook the lea ;
Pursue thy loves among the bowers,
 But leave thou mine to me.   200

O flourish, hidden deep in fern,
 Old oak, I love thee well ;
A thousand thanks for what I learn
 And what remains to tell.

' 'T is little more : the day was warm ;
 At last, tired out with play,
She sank her head upon her arm,
 And at my feet she lay.

' Her eyelids dropp'd their silken eaves.
 I breathed upon her eyes   210
Thro' all the summer of my leaves
 A welcome mix'd with sighs.

' I took the swarming sound of life —
 The music from the town —
The murmurs of the drum and fife,
 And lull'd them in my own.

' Sometimes I let a sunbeam slip,
 To light her shaded eye ;
A second flutter'd round her lip
 Like a golden butterfly ;   220

' A third would glimmer on her neck
 To make the necklace shine ;
Another slid, a sunny fleck,
 From head to ankle fine.

' Then close and dark my arms I spread,
 And shadow'd all her rest —
Dropt dews upon her golden head,
 An acorn in her breast.

'But in a pet she started up,
　　And pluck'd it out, and drew
My little oakling from the cup,
　　And flung him in the dew.

'And yet it was a graceful gift —
　　I felt a pang within
As when I see the woodman lift
　　His axe to slay my kin.

'I shook him down because he was
　　The finest on the tree.
He lies beside thee on the grass.
　　O kiss him once for me!

'O kiss him twice and thrice for me,
　　That have no lips to kiss,
For never yet was oak on lea
　　Shall grow so fair as this!'

Step deeper yet in herb and fern,
　　Look further thro' the chace,
Spread upward till thy boughs discern
　　The front of Sumner-place.

This fruit of thine by Love is blest,
　　That but a moment lay
Where fairer fruit of Love may rest
　　Some happy future day.

I kiss it twice, I kiss it thrice;
　　The warmth it thence shall win
To riper life may magnetize
　　The baby-oak within.

But thou, while kingdoms overset
 Or lapse from hand to hand,
Thy leaf shall never fail, nor yet
 Thine acorn in the land.

May never saw dismember thee,
 Nor wielded axe disjoint ;
That art the fairest-spoken tree
 From here to Lizard-point.

O rock upon thy towery top
 All throats that gurgle sweet !
All starry culmination drop
 Balm-dews to bathe thy feet !

All grass of silky feather grow —
 And while he sinks or swells
The full south-breeze around thee blow
 The sound of minster bells !

The fat earth feed thy branchy root,
 That under deeply strikes !
The northern morning o'er thee shoot,
 High up, in silver spikes !

Nor ever lightning char thy grain,
 But, rolling as in sleep,
Low thunders bring the mellow rain,
 That makes thee broad and deep !

And hear me swear a solemn oath,
 That only by thy side
Will I to Olive plight my troth,
 And gain her for my bride.

And when my marriage morn may fall,
   She, Dryad-like, shall wear
Alternate leaf and acorn-ball
   In wreath about her hair.

And I will work in prose and rhyme,
   And praise thee more in both
Than bard has honor'd beech or lime,
   Or that Thessalian growth,

In which the swarthy ringdove sat,
  And mystic sentence spoke ;
And more than England honors that,
  Thy famous brother-oak,

Wherein the younger Charles abode
  Till all the paths were dim,
And far below the Roundhead rode,
  And humm'd a surly hymn.   300

ULYSSES.

It little profits that an idle king,
By this still hearth, among these barren crags,
Match'd with an aged wife, I mete and dole
Unequal laws unto a savage race,
That hoard, and sleep, and feed, and know not me.
I cannot rest from travel ; I will drink
Life to the lees : all times I have enjoy'd
Greatly, have suffer'd greatly, both with those

That loved me, and alone ; on shore, and when
Thro' scudding drifts the rainy Hyades   10
Vext the dim sea.   I am become a name ;
For always roaming with a hungry heart
Much have I seen and known — cities of men
And manners, climates, councils, governments,
Myself not least, but honor'd of them all —
And drunk delight of battle with my peers,
Far on the ringing plains of windy Troy.
I am a part of all that I have met ;
Yet all experience is an arch wherethro'
Gleams that untravell'd world, whose margin fades   20
Forever and forever when I move.
How dull it is to pause, to make an end,
To rust unburnish'd, not to shine in use !
As tho' to breathe were life.   Life piled on life
Were all too little, and of one to me
Little remains : but every hour is saved
From that eternal silence, something more,
A bringer of new things ; and vile it were
For some three suns to store and hoard myself,
And this gray spirit yearning in desire   30
To follow knowledge like a sinking star,
Beyond the utmost bound of human thought.
   This is my son, mine own Telemachus,
To whom I leave the sceptre and the isle —
Well-loved of me, discerning to fulfil
This labor, by slow prudence to make mild
A rugged people, and thro' soft degrees
Subdue them to the useful and the good.
Most blameless is he, centred in the sphere
Of common duties, decent not to fail   40
In offices of tenderness, and pay
Meet adoration to my household gods,
When I am gone.   He works his work, I mine.

There lies the port : the vessel puffs her sail :
There gloom the dark broad seas.   My mariners,
Souls that have toil'd, and wrought, and thought with me —-
That ever with a frolic welcome took
The thunder and the sunshine, and opposed
Free hearts, free foreheads — you and I are old ;
Old age hath yet his honor and his toil ;
Death closes all : but something ere the end,
Some work of noble note, may yet be done,
Not unbecoming men that strove with Gods.
The lights begin to twinkle from the rocks ;
The long day wanes ; the slow moon climbs ; the deep
Moans round with many voices.   Come, my friends,
'T is not too late to seek a newer world.
Push off, and sitting well in order smite
The sounding furrows ; for my purpose holds
To sail beyond the sunset, and the baths
Of all the western stars, until I die.
It may be that the gulfs will wash us down ;
It may be we shall touch the Happy Isles,
And see the great Achilles, whom we knew.
Tho' much is taken, much abides ; and tho'
We are not now that strength which in old days
Moved earth and heaven, that which we are, we are ;
One equal temper of heroic hearts,
Made weak by time and fate, but strong in will
To strive, to seek, to find, and not to yield.

LOCKSLEY HALL.

COMRADES, leave me here a little, while as yet 't is early morn ;
Leave me here, and when you want me sound upon the bugle
   horn.

'T is the place, and all around it, as of old, the curlews call,
Dreary gleams about the moorland flying over Locksley Hall ;

Locksley Hall, that in the distance overlooks the sandy tracts,
And the hollow ocean-ridges roaring into cataracts.

Many a night from yonder ivied casement, ere I went to rest,
Did I look on great Orion sloping slowly to the West.

Many a night I saw the Pleiads, rising thro' the mellow shade,
Glitter like a swarm of fire-flies tangled in a silver braid.   10

Here about the beach I wander'd, nourishing a youth sublime
With the fairy tales of science, and the long result of Time ;

7

When the centuries behind me like a fruitful land reposed ;
When I clung to all the present for the promise that it closed :

When I dipt into the future far as human eye could see ;
Saw the vision of the world, and all the wonder that would
　　be. —

In the Spring a fuller crimson comes upon the robin's breast ;
In the Spring the wanton lapwing gets himself another crest ;

In the Spring a livelier iris changes on the burnish'd dove ;
In the Spring a young man's fancy lightly turns to thoughts
　　of love.　　　　　　　　　　　　　　　　　　　20

Then her cheek was pale and thinner than should be for one
　　so young,
And her eyes on all my motions with a mute observance hung.

And I said, ' My cousin Amy, speak, and speak the truth to
　　me ;
Trust me, cousin, all the current of my being sets to thee.'

On her pallid cheek and forehead came a color and a light,
As I have seen the rosy red flushing in the northern night.

And she turn'd — her bosom shaken with a sudden storm of
　　sighs —
All the spirit deeply dawning in the dark of hazel eyes —

Saying, ' I have hid my feelings, fearing they should do me
　　wrong ; '
Saying, ' Dost thou love me, cousin ? ' weeping, ' I have loved
　　thee long.'　　　　　　　　　　　　　　　　30

Love took up the glass of Time, and turn'd it in his glowing
    hands ;
Every moment, lightly shaken, ran itself in golden sands.

Love took up the harp of Life, and smote on all the chords
    with might ;
Smote the chord of Self, that, trembling, past in music out of
    sight.

Many a morning on the moorland did we hear the copses ring,
And her whisper throng'd my pulses with the fulness of the
    Spring.

Many an evening by the waters did we watch the stately ships,
And our spirits rush'd together at the touching of the lips.

O my cousin, shallow-hearted ! O my Amy, mine no more !
O the dreary, dreary moorland ! O the barren, barren
    shore !   40

Falser than all fancy fathoms, falser than all songs have sung,
Puppet to a father's threat, and servile to a shrewish tongue !

Is it well to wish thee happy ? — having known me — to decline
On a range of lower feelings and a narrower heart than mine !

Yet it shall be ; thou shalt lower to his level day by day,
What is fine within thee growing coarse to sympathize with
    clay.

As the husband is, the wife is ; thou art mated with a clown,
And the grossness of his nature will have weight to drag thee
    down.

He will hold thee, when his passion shall have spent its novel
    force,
Something better than his dog, a little dearer than his horse. 50

What is this? his eyes are heavy: think not they are glazed
    with wine.
Go to him; it is thy duty: kiss him; take his hand in thine.

It may be my lord is weary, that his brain is overwrought;
Soothe him with thy finer fancies, touch him with thy lighter
    thought.

He will answer to the purpose, easy things to understand —
Better thou wert dead before me, tho' I slew thee with my
    hand!

Better thou and I were lying, hidden from the heart's disgrace,
Roll'd in one another's arms, and silent in a last embrace.

Cursed be the social wants that sin against the strength of
    youth!
Cursed be the social lies that warp us from the living truth! 60

Cursed be the sickly forms that err from honest Nature's rule!
Cursed be the gold that gilds the straiten'd forehead of the
    fool!

Well — 't is well that I should bluster! — Hadst thou less un-
    worthy proved —
Would to God — for I had loved thee more than ever wife
    was loved.

Am I mad, that I should cherish that which bears but bitter
    fruit?
I will pluck it from my bosom, tho' my heart be at the root.

Never, tho' my mortal summers to such length of years should
    come
As the many-winter'd crow that leads the clanging rookery
    home.

Where is comfort? in division of the records of the mind?
Can I part her from herself, and love her, as I knew her,
    kind?   70

I remember one that perish'd; sweetly did she speak and
    move :
Such a one do I remember, whom to look at was to love.

Can I think of her as dead, and love her for the love she
    bore?
No — she never loved me truly; love is love forevermore.

Comfort? comfort scorn'd of devils! this is truth the poet
    sings,
That a sorrow's crown of sorrow is remembering happier
    things.

Drug thy memories, lest thou learn it, lest thy heart be put to
    proof,
In the dead unhappy night, and when the rain is on the roof.

Like a dog, he hunts in dreams, and thou art staring at the
    wall,
Where the dying night-lamp flickers, and the shadows rise and
    fall.   80

Then a hand shall pass before thee, pointing to his drunken
    sleep,
To thy widow'd marriage-pillows, to the tears that thou wilt
    weep.

Thou shalt hear the 'Never, never,' whisper'd by the phantom
    years,
And a song from out the distance in the ringing of thine ears ;

And an eye shall vex thee, looking ancient kindness on thy
    pain.
Turn thee, turn thee on thy pillow ; get thee to thy rest again.

Nay, but Nature brings thee solace ; for a tender voice will
    cry.
'T is a purer life than thine ; a lip to drain thy trouble dry.

Baby lips will laugh me down ; my latest rival brings thee rest.
Baby fingers, waxen touches, press me from the mother's
    breast.   90

O, the child too clothes the father with a dearness not his due.
Half is thine and half is his ; it will be worthy of the two.

O, I see thee old and formal, fitted to thy petty part,
With a little hoard of maxims preaching down a daughter's
    heart.

'They were dangerous guides the feelings — she herself was
    not exempt —
Truly, she herself had suffer'd ' — Perish in thy self-contempt !

Overlive it — lower yet — be happy ! wherefore should I care ?
I myself must mix with action, lest I wither by despair.

What is that which I should turn to, lighting upon days like
    these ?
Every door is barr'd with gold, and opens but to golden
    keys.   100

Every gate is throng'd with suitors, all the markets overflow.
I have but an angry fancy : what is that which I should do?

I had been content to perish, falling on the foeman's ground,
When the ranks are roll'd in vapor, and the winds are laid
    with sound.

But the jingling of the guinea helps the hurt that Honor feels,
And the nations do but murmur, snarling at each other's heels.

Can I but relive in sadness?   I will turn that earlier page.
Hide me from my deep emotion, O thou wondrous Mother-
    Age !

Make me feel the wild pulsation that I felt before the strife,
When I heard my days before me, and the tumult of my
    life ;   110

Yearning for the large excitement that the coming years would
    yield,
Eager-hearted as a boy when first he leaves his father's field,

And at night along the dusky highway, near and nearer drawn,
Sees in heaven the light of London flaring like a dreary dawn ;

And his spirit leaps within him to be gone before him then,
Underneath the light he looks at, in among the throngs of
    men ;

Men, my brothers, men the workers, ever reaping something
    new,
That which they have done but earnest of the things that they
    shall do :

For I dipt into the future, far as human eye could see,
Saw the vision of the world, and all the wonder that would
    be ;   120

Saw the heavens fill with commerce, argosies of magic sails,
Pilots of the purple twilight, dropping down with costly bales ;

Heard the heavens fill with shouting, and there rain'd a ghastly
    dew
From the nations' airy navies grappling in the central blue ;

Far along the world-wide whisper of the south-wind rushing
    warm,
With the standards of the peoples plunging thro' the thunder-
    storm ;

Till the war-drum throbb'd no longer, and the battle-flags were
    furl'd
In the Parliament of man, the Federation of the world.

There the common sense of most shall hold a fretful realm in
    awe,
And the kindly earth shall slumber, lapt in universal law.   130

So I triumph'd, ere my passion sweeping thro' me left me dry,
Left me with the palsied heart, and left me with the jaundiced
    eye ;

Eye, to which all order festers, all things here are out of joint ;
Science moves, but slowly slowly, creeping on from point to
    point ;

Slowly comes a hungry people, as a lion, creeping nigher,
Glares at one that nods and winks behind a slowly-dying fire.

Yet I doubt not thro' the ages one increasing purpose runs,
And the thoughts of men are widen'd with the process of the
suns.

What is that to him that reaps not harvest of his youthful joys,
Tho' the deep heart of existence beat forever like a boy's? 140

Knowledge comes, but wisdom lingers, and I linger on the
shore,
And the individual withers, and the world is more and more.

Knowledge comes, but wisdom lingers, and he bears a laden
breast,
Full of sad experience, moving toward the stillness of his rest.

Hark, my merry comrades call me, sounding on the bugle-
horn,
They to whom my foolish passion were a target for their
scorn :

Shall it not be scorn to me to harp on such a moulder'd
string?
I am shamed thro' all my nature to have loved so slight a
thing.

Weakness to be wroth with weakness! woman's pleasure,
woman's pain —
Nature made them blinder motions bounded in a shallower
brain : 150

Woman is the lesser man, and all thy passions, match'd with
mine,
Are as moonlight unto sunlight, and as water unto wine —

Here at least, where nature sickens, nothing.　Ah, for some
　　retreat
Deep in yonder shining Orient, where my life began to beat ;

Where in wild Mahratta-battle fell my father evil-starr'd ; —
I was left a trampled orphan, and a selfish uncle's ward.

Or to burst all links of habit — there to wander far away,
On from island unto island at the gateways of the day.

Larger constellations burning, mellow moons and happy skies,
Breadths of tropic shade and palms in cluster, knots of
　　Paradise.　　　　　　　　　　　　　　　　　160

Never comes the trader, never floats an European flag,
Slides the bird o'er lustrous woodland, swings the trailer from
　　the crag ;

Droops the heavy-blossom'd bower, hangs the heavy-fruited
　　tree —
Summer isles of Eden lying in dark-purple spheres of sea.

There methinks would be enjoyment more than in this march
　　of mind,
In the steamship, in the railway, in the thoughts that shake
　　mankind.

There the passions cramp'd no longer shall have scope and
　　breathing-space :
I will take some savage woman, she shall rear my dusky race.

Iron-jointed, supple-sinew'd, they shall dive, and they shall run,
Catch the wild goat by the hair, and hurl their lances in the
　　sun ;　　　　　　　　　　　　　　　　　170

Whistle back the parrot's call, and leap the rainbows of the
    brooks,
Not with blinded eyesight poring over miserable books —

Fool, again the dream, the fancy ! but I *know* my words are
    wild,
But I count the gray barbarian lower than the Christian child.

I, to herd with narrow foreheads, vacant of our glorious gains,
Like a beast with lower pleasures, like a beast with lower
    pains !

Mated with a squalid savage — what to me were sun or clime ?
I the heir of all the ages, in the foremost files of time —

I that rather held it better men should perish one by one,
Than that earth should stand at gaze like Joshua's moon in
    Ajalon !   180

Not in vain the distance beacons. Forward, forward let us
    range.
Let the great world spin forever down the ringing grooves of
    change.

Thro' the shadow of the globe we sweep into the younger day :
Better fifty years of Europe than a cycle of Cathay.

Mother-Age (for mine I knew not) help me as when life begun ;
Rift the hills, and roll the waters, flash the lightnings, weigh
    the sun —

O, I see the crescent promise of my spirit hath not set.
Ancient founts of inspiration well thro' all my fancy yet.

Howsoever these things be, a long farewell to Locksley Hall !
Now for me the woods may wither, now for me the roof-tree
    fall.   190

Comes a vapor from the margin, blackening over heath and
    holt,
Cramming all the blast before it, in its breast a thunderbolt.

Let it fall on Locksley Hall, with rain or hail, or fire or snow ;
For the mighty wind arises, roaring seaward, and I go.

—◆◇◆—

THE TWO VOICES.

A STILL small voice spake unto me,
'Thou art so full of misery,
Were it not better not to be ? '

Then to the still small voice I said :
' Let me not cast in endless shade
What is so wonderfully made.'

To which the voice did urge reply :
' To-day I saw the dragon-fly
Come from the wells where he did lie.

' An inner impulse rent the veil   10
Of his old husk ; from head to tail
Came out clear plates of sapphire mail.

' He dried his wings ; like gauze they grew :
Thro' crofts and pastures wet with dew
A living flash of light he flew.'

I said, 'When first the world began,
Young Nature thro' five cycles ran,
And in the sixth she moulded man.

'She gave him mind, the lordliest
Proportion, and, above the rest,　　　　　20
Dominion in the head and breast.'

Thereto the silent voice replied :
'Self-blinded are you by your pride :
Look up thro' night : the world is wide.

'This truth within thy mind rehearse,
That in a boundless universe
Is boundless better, boundless worse.

'Think you this mould of hopes and fears
Could find no statelier than his peers
In yonder hundred million spheres?'　　　30

It spake, moreover, in my mind :
'Tho' thou wert scatter'd to the wind,
Yet is there plenty of the kind.'

Then did my response clearer fall :
'No compound of this earthly ball
Is like another, all in all.'

To which he answer'd scoffingly :
'Good soul ! suppose I grant it thee,
Who 'll weep for thy deficiency?

'Or will one beam be less intense,　　　40
When thy peculiar difference
Is cancell'd in the world of sense?'

I would have said, 'Thou canst not know,'
But my full heart, that work'd below,
Rain'd thro' my sight its overflow.

Again the voice spake unto me :
'Thou art so steep'd in misery,
Surely, 't were better not to be.

' Thine anguish will not let thee sleep,
Nor any train of reason keep ;
Thou canst not think but thou wilt weep.'

I said, ' The years with change advance :
If I make dark my countenance,
I shut my life from happier chance.

' Some turn this sickness yet might take,
Even yet.'   But he : ' What drug can make
A wither'd palsy cease to shake ? '

I wept, ' Tho' I should die, I know
That all about the thorn will blow
In tufts of rosy-tinted snow ;

' And men, thro' novel spheres of thought
Still moving after truth long sought,
Will learn new things when I am not.'

' Yet,' said the secret voice, ' some time
Sooner or later, will gray prime
Make thy grass hoar with early rime.

' Not less swift souls that yearn for light,
Rapt after heaven's starry flight,
Would sweep the tracts of day and night.

'Not less the bee would range her cells,   70
The furzy prickle fire the dells,
The foxglove cluster dappled bells.'

I said that 'all the years invent;
Each month is various to present
The world with some development.

'Were this not well, to bide mine hour,
Tho' watching from a ruin'd tower
How grows the day of human power?'

'The highest-mounted mind,' he said,
'Still sees the sacred morning spread   80
The silent summit overhead.

'Will thirty seasons render plain
Those lonely lights that still remain,
Just breaking over land and main?

'Or make that morn, from his cold crown
And crystal silence creeping down,
Flood with full daylight glebe and town?

'Forerun thy peers, thy time, and let
Thy feet, millenniums hence, be set
In midst of knowledge dream'd not yet.   90

'Thou hast not gained a real height,
Nor art thou nearer to the light,
Because the scale is infinite.

''Twere better not to breathe or speak,
Than cry for strength, remaining weak,
And seem to find, but still to seek.

'Moreover, but to seem to find
Asks what thou lackest, thought resign'd,
A healthy frame, a quiet mind.'

I said, 'When I am gone away,
"He dared not tarry," men will say,
Doing dishonor to my clay.'

'This is more vile,' he made reply,
'To breathe and loathe, to live and sigh,
Than once from dread of pain to die.

'Sick art thou — a divided will
Still heaping on the fear of ill
The fear of men, a coward still.

'Do men love thee?   Art thou so bound
To men, that how thy name may sound
Will vex thee lying underground?

'The memory of the wither'd leaf
In endless time is scarce more brief
Than of the garner'd Autumn-sheaf.

'Go, vexed Spirit, sleep in trust ;
The right ear that is fill'd with dust
Hears little of the false or just.'

'Hard task, to pluck resolve,' I cried,
'From emptiness and the waste wide
Of that abyss, or scornful pride !

'Nay — rather yet that I could raise
One hope that warm'd me in the days
While still I yearn'd for human praise.

'When, wide in soul and bold of tongue,
Among the tents I paused and sung,
The distant battle flash'd and rung.

'I sung the joyful Pæan clear,
And, sitting, burnish'd without fear
The brand, the buckler, and the spear —

'Waiting to strive a happy strife,   130
To war with falsehood to the knife,
And not to lose the good of life —

'Some hidden principle to move,
To put together, part and prove,
And mete the bounds of hate and love —

'As far as might be, to carve out
Free space for every human doubt,
That the whole mind might orb about —

'To search thro' all I felt or saw,
The springs of life, the depths of awe,   140
And reach the law within the law :

'At least, not rotting like a weed,
But, having sown some generous seed,
Fruitful of further thought and deed,

'To pass, when Life her light withdraws,
Not void of righteous self-applause,
Nor in a merely selfish cause —

'In some good cause, not in mine own,
To perish, wept for, honor'd, known,
And like a warrior overthrown ;   150

8

'Whose eyes are dim with glorious tears,
When, soil'd with noble dust, he hears
His country's war-song thrill his ears:

'Then dying of a mortal stroke,
What time the foeman's line is broke,
And all the war is roll'd in smoke.'

'Yea!' said the voice, 'thy dream was good,
While thou abodest in the bud.
It was the stirring of the blood.

'If Nature put not forth her power   160
About the opening of the flower,
Who is it that could live an hour?

'Then comes the check, the change, the fall.
Pain rises up, old pleasures pall.
There is one remedy for all.

'Yet hadst thou, thro' enduring pain,
Link'd month to month with such a chain
Of knitted purport, all were vain.

'Thou hadst not between death and birth
Dissolved the riddle of the earth.   170
So were thy labor little-worth.

'That men with knowledge merely play'd,
I told thee — hardly nigher made,
Tho' scaling slow from grade to grade;

'Much less this dreamer, deaf and blind,
Named man, may hope some truth to find
That bears relation to the mind.

'For every worm beneath the moon
Draws different threads, and late and soon
Spins, toiling out his own cocoon.   180

'Cry, faint not: either Truth is born
Beyond the polar gleam forlorn,
Or in the gateways of the morn.

'Cry, faint not, climb: the summits slope
Beyond the furthest flights of hope,
Wrapt in dense cloud from base to cope.

'Sometimes a little corner shines,
As over rainy mist inclines
A gleaming crag with belts of pines.

'I will go forward, sayest thou,   190
I shall not fail to find her now.
Look up, the fold is on her brow.

'If straight thy tract, or if oblique,
Thou know'st not.   Shadows thou dost strike,
Embracing cloud, Ixion-like;

'And owning but a little more
Than beasts, abidest lame and poor,
Calling thyself a little lower

'Than angels.   Cease to wail and brawl!
Why inch by inch to darkness crawl?   200
There is one remedy for all.'

'O dull, one-sided voice,' said I,
'Wilt thou make everything a lie,
To flatter me that I may die?

'I know that age to age succeeds,
Blowing a noise of tongues and deeds,
A dust of systems and of creeds.

'I cannot hide that some have striven,
Achieving calm, to whom was given
The joy that mixes man with Heaven :   21

'Who, rowing hard against the stream,
Saw distant gates of Eden gleam,
And did not dream it was a dream ;

'But heard, by secret transport led,
Even in the charnels of the dead,
The murmur of the fountain-head —

'Which did accomplish their desire,
Bore and forbore, and did not tire,
Like Stephen, an unquenched fire.

'He heeded not reviling tones,   22
Nor sold his heart to idle moans,
Tho' curs'd and scorn'd, and bruised with stones :

'But looking upward, full of grace,
He pray'd, and from a happy place
God's glory smote him on the face.'

The sullen answer slid betwixt :
'Not that the grounds of hope were fixt,
The elements were kindlier mixt.'

I said, 'I toil beneath the curse,
But, knowing not the universe,   23
I fear to slide from bad to worse ;

'And that, in seeking to undo
One riddle, and to find the true,
I knit a hundred others new;

'Or that this anguish fleeting hence,
Unmanacled from bonds of sense,
Be fixt and frozen to permanence:

'For I go, weak from suffering here;
Naked I go, and void of cheer:
What is it that I may not fear?' 240

'Consider well,' the voice replied,
'His face, that two hours since hath died;
Wilt thou find passion, pain, or pride?

'Will he obey when one commands?
Or answer should one press his hands?
He answers not, nor understands.

'His palms are folded on his breast:
There is no other thing exprest
But long disquiet merged in rest.

'His lips are very mild and meek: 250
Tho' one should smite him on the cheek,
And on the mouth, he will not speak.

'His little daughter, whose sweet face
He kiss'd, taking his last embrace,
Becomes dishonor to her race —

'His sons grow up that bear his name,
Some grow to honor, some to shame, —
But he is chill to praise or blame.

'He will not hear the north-wind rave,
Nor, moaning, household shelter crave
From winter rains that beat his grave.

'High up the vapors fold and swim ;
About him broods the twilight dim ;
The place he knew forgetteth him.'

'If all be dark, vague voice,' I said,
'These things are wrapt in doubt and dread,
Nor canst thou show the dead are dead.

'The sap dries up ; the plant declines.
A deeper tale my heart divines.
Know I not Death? the outward signs?

'I found him when my years were few ;
A shadow on the graves I knew,
And darkness in the village yew.

'From grave to grave the shadow crept ;
In her still place the morning wept ;
Touch'd by his feet the daisy slept.

'The simple senses crown'd his head :
"Omega ! thou art Lord," they said,
"We find no motion in the dead."

'Why, if man rot in dreamless ease,
Should that plain fact, as taught by these,
Not make him sure that he shall cease?

'Who forged that other influence,
That heat of inward evidence,
By which he doubts against the sense?

'He owns the fatal gift of eyes,
That read his spirit blindly wise,
Not simple as a thing that dies.

'Here sits he shaping wings to fly;
His heart forebodes a mystery;   290
He names the name Eternity.

'That type of Perfect in his mind
In Nature can he nowhere find.
He sows himself on every wind.

'He seems to hear a Heavenly Friend,
And thro' thick veils to apprehend
A labor working to an end.

'The end and the beginning vex
His reason; many things perplex,
With motions, checks, and counter-checks.   300

'He knows a baseness in his blood
At such strange war with something good,
He may not do the thing he would.

'Heaven opens inward, chasms yawn,
Vast images in glimmering dawn,
Half-shown, are broken and withdrawn.

'Ah! sure within him and without,
Could his dark wisdom find it out,
There must be answer to his doubt.

'But thou canst answer not again.   310
With thine own weapon art thou slain,
Or thou wilt answer but in vain.

''The doubt would rest, I dare not solve.
In the same circle we revolve.
Assurance only breeds resolve.'

As when a billow, blown against,
Falls back, the voice with which I fenced
A little ceased, but recommenced :

'Where wert thou when thy father play'd
In his free field, and pastime made,
A merry boy in sun and shade ?

'A merry boy they called him then.
He sat upon the knees of men
In days that never come again.

'Before the little ducts began
To feed thy bones with lime, and ran
Their course, till thou wert also man :

'Who took a wife, who rear'd his race,
Whose wrinkles gather'd on his face,
Whose troubles number with his days ;

'A life of nothings, nothing-worth,
From that first nothing ere his birth
To that last nothing under earth ! '

'These words,' I said, 'are like the rest ;
No certain clearness, but at best
A vague suspicion of the breast :

'But if I grant, thou might'st defend
The thesis which thy words intend —
That to begin implies to end ;

'Yet how should I for certain hold,   340
Because my memory is so cold,
That I first was in human mould?

'I cannot make this matter plain,
But I would shoot, howe'er in vain,
A random arrow from the brain.

'It may be that no life is found,
Which only to one engine bound
Falls off, but cycles always round.

'As old mythologies relate,
Some draught of Lethe might await   350
The slipping thro' from state to state ;

'As here we find in trances, men
Forget the dream that happens then,
Until they fall in trance again :

'So might we, if our state were such
As one before, remember much,
For those two likes might meet and touch.

'But, if I lapsed from nobler place,
Some legend of a fallen race
Alone might hint of my disgrace ;   360

'Some vague emotion of delight
In gazing up an Alpine height,
Some yearning toward the lamps of night.

'Or if thro' lower lives I came —
Tho' all experience past became
Consolidate in mind and frame —

' I might forget my weaker lot ;
For is not our first year forgot ?
The haunts' of memory echo not.

' And men, whose reason long was blind,
From cells of madness unconfined,
Oft lose whole years of darker mind.

' Much more, if first I floated free,
As naked essence, must I be
Incompetent of memory ;

' For memory dealing but with time,
And he with matter, could she climb
Beyond her own material prime ?

' Moreover, something is or seems,
That touches me with mystic gleams,
Like glimpses of forgotten dreams —

' Of something felt, like something here ;
Of something done, I know not where ;
Such as no language may declare.'

The still voice laugh'd.   ' I talk,' said he,
' Not with thy dreams.   Suffice it thee
Thy pain is a reality.'

' But thou,' said I, ' hast miss'd thy mark,
Who sought'st to wreck my mortal ark,
By making all the horizon dark.

' Why not set forth, if I should do
This rashness, that which might ensue
With this old soul in organs new ?

'Whatever crazy sorrow saith,
No life that breathes with human breath
Has ever truly long'd for death.

' 'T is life whereof our nerves are scant,
O life, not death, for which we pant ;
More life, and fuller, that I want.'

I ceased, and sat as one forlorn.　　　　　　400
Then said the voice, in quiet scorn :
'Behold, it is the Sabbath morn.'

And I arose, and I released
The casement, and the light increased
With freshness in the dawning east.

Like soften'd airs that blowing steal,
When meres begin to uncongeal,
The sweet church bells began to peal.

On to God's house the people prest :
Passing the place where each must rest,　　　　410
Each enter'd like a welcome guest.

One walk'd between his wife and child,
With measur'd footfall firm and mild,
And now and then he gravely smiled.

The prudent partner of his blood
Lean'd on him, faithful, gentle, good,
Wearing the rose of womanhood.

And in their double love secure,
The little maiden walk'd demure,
Pacing with downward eyelids pure.　　　　420

These three made unity so sweet,
My frozen heart began to beat,
Remembering its ancient heat.

I blest them, and they wander'd on :
I spoke, but answer came there none ;
The dull and bitter voice was gone.

A second voice was at mine ear,
A little whisper silver-clear,
A murmur, ' Be of better cheer.'

As from some blissful neighborhood,   430
A notice faintly understood,
' I see the end, and know the good.

A little hint to solace woe,
A hint, a whisper breathing low,
' I may not speak of what I know.'

Like an Æolian harp that wakes
No certain air, but overtakes
Far thought with music that it makes :

Such seem'd the whisper at my side :
' What is it thou knowest, sweet voice ? ' I cried.   410
' A hidden hope,' the voice replied ;

So heavenly-toned, that in that hour
From out my sullen heart a power
Broke, like the rainbow from the shower,

To feel, altho' no tongue can prove,
That every cloud, that spreads above
And veileth love, itself is love.

And forth into the fields I went,
And Nature's living motion lent
The pulse of hope to discontent.   450

I wonder'd at the bounteous hours,
The slow result of winter-showers :
You scarce could see the grass for flowers.

I wonder'd, while I paced along :
The woods were fill'd so full with song,
There seem'd no room for sense of wrong ;

And all so variously wrought,
I marvell'd how the mind was brought
To anchor by one gloomy thought ;

And wherefore rather I made choice   460
To commune with that barren voice,
Than him that said, 'Rejoice ! rejoice ! '

ST. AGNES' EVE.

DEEP on the convent-roof the snows
    Are sparkling to the moon :
My breath to heaven like vapor goes ;
    May my soul follow soon !
The shadows of the convent-towers
    Slant down the snowy sward,
Still creeping with the creeping hours
    That lead me to my Lord :
Make Thou my spirit pure and clear
    As are the frosty skies,   10
Or this first snowdrop of the year
    That in my bosom lies.

As these white robes are soil'd and dark,
    To yonder shining ground ;
As this pale taper's earthly spark,
    To yonder argent round ;
So shows my soul before the Lamb,
    My spirit before Thee ;

So in mine earthly house I am,
 To that I hope to be.
Break up the heavens, O Lord ! and far,
 Thro' all yon starlight keen,
Draw me, thy bride, a glittering star,
 In raiment white and clean.

20

He lifts me to the golden doors :
   The flashes come and go ;
All heaven bursts her starry floors,
   And strews her lights below,
And deepens on and up ! the gates
   Roll back, and far within
For me the Heavenly Bridegroom waits,
   To make me pure of sin.
The sabbaths of Eternity,
   One sabbath deep and wide —
A light upon the shining sea —
   The Bridegroom with his bride !

SIR GALAHAD.

My good blade carves the casques of men,
   My tough lance thrusteth sure,
My strength is as the strength of ten,
   Because my heart is pure.
The shattering trumpet shrilleth high,
   The hard brands shiver on the steel,
The splinter'd spear-shafts crack and fly,
   The horse and rider reel ;
They reel, they roll in clanging lists,
   And when the tide of combat stands,
Perfume and flowers fall in showers,
   That lightly rain from ladies' hands.

How sweet are looks that ladies bend
   On whom their favors fall !
For them I battle to the end,
   To save from shame and thrall :

But all my heart is drawn above,
  My knees are bow'd in crypt and shrine ;
I never felt the kiss of love,
  Nor maiden's hand in mine.   **20**
More bounteous aspects on me beam,
  Me mightier transports move and thrill ;
So keep I fair thro' faith and prayer
  A virgin heart in work and will.

When down the stormy crescent goes,
 A light before me swims,
Between dark stems the forest glows,
 I hear a noise of hymns:
Then by some secret shrine I ride;
 I hear a voice, but none are there; 30
The stalls are void, the doors are wide,
 The tapers burning fair.
Fair gleams the snowy altar-cloth,
 The silver vessels sparkle clean,
The shrill bell rings, the censer swings,
 And solemn chants resound between.

Sometimes on lonely mountain-meres
 I find a magic bark;
I leap on board: no helmsman steers:
 I float till all is dark. 40
A gentle sound, an awful light!
 Three angels bear the Holy Grail:
With folded feet, in stoles of white,
 On sleeping wings they sail.
Ah, blessed vision! blood of God!
 My spirit beats her mortal bars,
As down dark tides the glory slides,
 And starlike mingles with the stars.

When on my goodly charger borne
 Thro' dreaming towns I go, 50
The cock crows ere the Christmas morn,
 The streets are dumb with snow.
The tempest crackles on the leads,
 And, ringing, spins from brand and mail;
But o'er the dark a glory spreads,
 And gilds the driving hail.

I leave the plain, I climb the height ;
  No branchy thicket shelter yields :
But blessed forms in whistling storms
  Fly o'er waste fens and windy fields.   60

A maiden knight — to me is given
  Such hope, I know not fear ;
I yearn to breathe the airs of heaven
  That often meet me here.
I muse on joy that will not cease,
  Pure spaces clothed in living beams,
Pure lilies of eternal peace,
  Whose odors haunt my dreams ;
And, stricken by an angel's hand,
  This mortal armor that I wear,   70
This weight and size, this heart and eyes,
  Are touch'd, are turn'd to finest air.

The clouds are broken in the sky,
  And thro' the mountain-walls
A rolling organ-harmony
  Swells up, and shakes and falls.
Then move the trees, the copses nod,
  Wings flutter, voices hover clear :
'O just and faithful knight of God !
  Ride on ! the prize is near.'   80
So pass I hostel, hall, and grange ;
  By bridge and ford, by park and pale,
All-arm'd I ride, whate'er betide,
  Until I find the Holy Grail.

THE BROOK;

AN IDYL.

'Here, by this brook, we parted; I to the East
And he for Italy — too late — too late :
One whom the strong sons of the world despise ;
For lucky rhymes to him were scrip and share,
And mellow metres more than cent for cent ;

Nor could he understand how money breeds,
Thought it a dead thing ; yet himself could make
The thing that is not as the thing that is.
O had he lived !   In our schoolbooks we say,
Of those that held their heads above the crowd,   10
They flourish'd then or then ; but life in him
Could scarce be said to flourish, only touch'd
On such a time as goes before the leaf,
When all the wood stands in a mist of green,
And nothing perfect : yet the brook he loved,
For which, in branding summers of Bengal,
Or even the sweet half-English Neilgherry air,
I panted, seems, as I re-listen to it,
Prattling the primrose fancies of the boy
To me that loved him ; for " O brook," he says,   20
" O babbling brook," says Edmund in his rhyme,
" Whence come you ? " and the brook, why not ? replies :

I come from haunts of coot and hern,
    I make a sudden sally
And sparkle out among the fern,
    To bicker down a valley.

By thirty hills I hurry down,
    Or slip between the ridges,
By twenty thorps, a little town,
    And half a hundred bridges.   30

Till last by Philip's farm I flow
    To join the brimming river,
For men may come and men may go,
    But I go on forever.

' Poor lad, he died at Florence, quite worn out,
Travelling to Naples.   There is Darnley bridge,
It has more ivy ; there the river ; and there
Stands Philip's farm where brook and river meet.

I chatter over stony ways,
    In little sharps and trebles,
I bubble into eddying bays,
    I babble on the pebbles.

With many a curve my banks I fret
    By many a field and fallow,
And many a fairy foreland set
    With willow-weed and mallow.

I chatter, chatter, as I flow
    To join the brimming river,
For men may come and men may go,
    But I go on forever.

' But Philip chatter'd more than brook or bird ;
Old Philip ; all about the fields you caught
His weary daylong chirping, like the dry
High-elbow'd grigs that leap in summer grass.

I wind about, and in and out,
    With here a blossom sailing,
And here and there a lusty trout,
    And here and there a grayling,

And here and there a foamy flake
    Upon me, as I travel,
With many a silver waterbreak
    Above the golden gravel,

And draw them all along, and flow
    To join the brimming river,
For men may come and men may go,
    But I go on forever.

' O darling Katie Willows, his one child !
A maiden of our century, yet most meek ;
A daughter of our meadows, yet not coarse ;

Straight, but as lissome as a hazel wand ;   70
Her eyes a bashful azure, and her hair
In gloss and hue the chestnut, when the shell
Divides threefold to show the fruit within.

'Sweet Katie, once I did her a good turn,
Her and her far-off cousin and betrothed, .
James Willows, of one name and heart with her.
For here I came, twenty years back, — the week
Before I parted with poor Edmund ; crost
By that old bridge which, half in ruins then,
Still makes a hoary eyebrow for the gleam   80
Beyond it; where the waters marry — crost,
Whistling a random bar of Bonny Doon,
And push'd at Philip's garden-gate.   The gate,
Half-parted from a weak and scolding hinge,
Stuck ; and he clamor'd from a casement, " Run,"
To Katie somewhere in the walks below,
" Run, Katie ! "   Katie never ran : she moved
To meet me, winding under woodbine bowers,
A little flutter'd with her eyelids down,
Fresh apple-blossom, blushing for a boon.   90

'What was it?   Less of sentiment than sense
Had Katie ; not illiterate ; neither one
Who babbling in the fount of fictive tears,
And nursed by mealy-mouthed philanthropies,
Divorce the Feeling from her mate the Deed.

'She told me.   She and James had quarrell'd.   Why?
What cause of quarrel?   None, she said, no cause ;
James had no cause : but when I prest the cause,
I learnt that James had flickering jealousies
Which anger'd her.   Who anger'd James? I said.   100
But Katie snatch'd her eyes at once from mine,

And sketching with her slender-pointed foot
Some figure like a wizard pentagram
On garden gravel, let my query pass
Unclaim'd, in flushing silence, till I ask'd
If James were coming.   " Coming every day,"
She answer'd, " ever longing to explain,
But evermore her father came across
With some long-winded tale, and broke him short ;
And James departed vext with him and her."   110
How could I help her?   " Would I — was it wrong?"
(Claspt hands and that petitionary grace
Of sweet seventeen subdued me ere she spoke)
" O would I take her father for one hour,
For one half-hour, and let him talk to me !"
And even while she spoke, I saw where James
Made towards us, like a wader in the surf,
Beyond the brook, waist-deep in meadow-sweet.

'O Katie, what I suffer'd for your sake !
For in I went and call'd old Philip out   120
To show the farm : full willingly he rose ;
He led me thro' the short sweet-smelling lanes
Of his wheat suburb, babbling as he went.
He prais'd his land, his horses, his machines ;
He prais'd his ploughs, his cows, his hogs, his dogs ;
He prais'd his hens, his geese, his guinea-hens ;
His pigeons, who in session on their roofs
Approved him, bowing at their own deserts :
Then from the plaintive mother's teat he took
Her blind and shuddering puppies, naming each,   130
And naming those, his friends, for whom they were :
Then crost the common into Darnley chase
To show Sir Arthur's deer.   In copse and fern
Twinkled the innumerable ear and tail.
Then, seated on a serpent-rooted beech,

He pointed out a pasturing colt, and said :
"That was the four-year-old I sold the squire."
And there he told a long, long-winded tale
Of how the squire had seen the colt at grass,
And how it was the thing his daughter wish'd,   140
And how he sent the bailiff to the farm
To learn the price, and what the price he ask'd,
And how the bailiff swore that he was mad,
But he stood firm ; and so the matter hung ;
He gave them line : and five days after that
He met the bailiff at the Golden Fleece,
Who then and there had offer'd something more,
But he stood firm ; and so the matter hung ;
He knew the man ; the colt would fetch its price ;
He gave them line : and how by chance at last   150
(It might be May or April, he forgot,
The last of April or the first of May)
He found the bailiff riding by the farm,
And, talking from the point, he drew him in,
And there he mellow'd all his heart with ale,
Until they closed a bargain, hand in hand.

'Then, while I breathed in sight of haven, he,
Poor fellow, could he help it? recommenced,
And ran thro' all the coltish chronicle,
Wild Will, Black Bess, Tantivy, Tallyho,   160
Reform, White Rose, Bellerophon, the Jilt,
Arbaces, and Phenomenon, and the rest,
Till, not to die a listener, I arose,
And with me Philip, talking still ; and so
We turn'd our foreheads from the falling sun,
And following our own shadows thrice as long
As when they follow'd us from Philip's door,
Arrived, and found the sun of sweet content
Re-risen in Katie's eyes, and all things well.

I steal by lawns and grassy plots,   170
   I slide by hazel covers ;
I move the sweet forget-me-nots
   That grow for happy lovers.

I slip, I slide, I gloom, I glance,
   Among my skimming swallows ;
I make the netted sunbeam dance
   Against my sandy shallows.

I murmur under moon and stars
   In brambly wildernesses ;
I linger by my shingly bars ;   180
   I loiter round my cresses ;

And out again I curve and flow
   To join the brimming river,
For men may come and men may go,
   But I go on forever.

Yes, men may come and go ; and these are gone,
All gone.   My dearest brother, Edmund, sleeps,
Not by the well-known stream and rustic spire,
But unfamiliar Arno, and the dome
Of Brunelleschi ; sleeps in peace : and he,   190
Poor Philip, of all his lavish waste of words
Remains the lean P. W. on his tomb :
I scraped the lichen from it : Katie walks
By the long wash of Australasian seas
Far off, and holds her head to other stars,
And breathes in converse seasons.   All are gone.'

   So Lawrence Aylmer, seated on a stile
In the long hedge, and rolling in his mind
Old waifs of rhyme, and bowing o'er the brook
A tonsured head in middle age forlorn,   200
Mused, and was mute.   On a sudden a low breath

Of tender air made tremble in the hedge
The fragile bindweed-bells and briony rings ;
And he look'd up.   There stood a maiden near,
Waiting to pass.   In much amaze he stared
On eyes a bashful azure, and on hair
In gloss and hue the chestnut, when the shell
Divides threefold to show the fruit within :
Then, wondering, ask'd her, 'Are you from the farm?'
'Yes,' answer'd she.   'Pray stay a little : pardon me ;   210
What do they call you?'   'Katie.'   'That were strange.
What   surname?'   'Willows.'   'No!'   'That is my
        name.'
'Indeed!' and here he look'd so self-perplext,
That Katie laugh'd, and laughing blush'd, till he
Laugh'd also, but as one before he wakes,
Who feels a glimmering strangeness in his dream.
Then looking at her : 'Too happy, fresh and fair,
Too fresh and fair in our sad world's best bloom,
To be the ghost of one who bore your name
About these meadows, twenty years ago.'   220

'Have you not heard?' said Katie, 'we came back.
We bought the farm we tenanted before.
Am I so like her? so they said on board.
Sir, if you knew her in her English days,
My mother, as it seems you did, the days
That most she loves to talk of, come with me.
My brother James is in the harvest-field :
But she — you will be welcome — O, come in !'

ODE ON THE DEATH OF THE DUKE OF WELLINGTON.

I.

Bury the Great Duke
　With an empire's lamentation,
Let us bury the Great Duke
　To the noise of the mourning of a mighty nation,
Mourning when their leaders fall,
Warriors carry the warrior's pall,
And sorrow darkens hamlet and hall.

II.

Where shall we lay the man whom we deplore?
Here, in streaming London's central roar.
Let the sound of those he wrought for,
And the feet of those he fought for,
Echo round his bones forevermore.

III.

Lead out the pageant : sad and slow,
As fits an universal woe,
Let the long long procession go,
And let the sorrowing crowd about it grow,
And let the mournful martial music blow ;
The last great Englishman is low.

IV.

Mourn, for to us he seems the last,
Remembering all his greatness in the past.   20
No more in soldier fashion will he greet
With lifted hand the gazer in the street.
O friends, our chief state-oracle is mute :
Mourn for the man of long-enduring blood,
The statesman-warrior, moderate, resolute,
Whole in himself, a common good.
Mourn for the man of amplest influence,
Yet clearest of ambitious crime,
Our greatest yet with least pretence,
Great in council and great in war,   30
Foremost captain of his time,
Rich in saving common-sense,
And, as the greatest only are,
In his simplicity sublime.
O good gray head which all men knew,
O voice from which their omens all men drew,
O iron nerve to true occasion true,
O fallen at length that tower of strength
Which stood four-square to all the winds that blew !
Such was he whom we deplore.   40
The long self-sacrifice of life is o'er.
The great World-victor's victor will be seen no more.

V.

All is over and done :
Render thanks to the Giver,
England, for thy son.
Let the bell be toll'd.
Render thanks to the Giver,
And render him to the mould.
Under the cross of gold
That shines over city and river,
There he shall rest forever
Among the wise and the bold.
Let the bell be toll'd,
And a reverent people behold
The towering car, the sable steeds :
Bright let it be with his blazon'd deeds,
Dark in its funeral fold.
Let the bell be toll'd :
And a deeper knell in the heart be knoll'd ;
And the sound of the sorrowing anthem roll'd
Thro' the dome of the golden cross ;
And the volleying cannon thunder his loss ;
He knew their voices of old.
For many a time in many a clime
His captain's-car has heard them boom
Bellowing victory, bellowing doom ;
When he with those deep voices wrought,
Guarding realms and kings from shame ;
With those deep voices our dead captain taught
The tyrant, and asserts his claim
In that dread sound to the great name,
Which he has worn so pure of blame,
In praise and in dispraise the same,
A man of well-attemper'd frame.
O civic muse, to such a name,

To such a name for ages long,
To such a name,
Preserve a broad approach of fame,
And ever-echoing avenues of song.

VI.

Who is he that cometh, like an honor'd guest,   80
With banner and with music, with soldier and with priest,
With a nation weeping, and breaking on my rest?
Mighty Seaman, this is he
Was great by land as thou by sea.
Thine island loves thee well, thou famous man,
The greatest sailor since our world began.
Now, to the roll of muffled drums,
To thee the greatest soldier comes ;
For this is he
Was great by land as thou by sea ;   90
His foes were thine ; he kept us free.
O give him welcome, this is he,
Worthy of our gorgeous rites,
And worthy to be laid by thee ;
For this is England's greatest son,
He that gain'd a hundred fights,
Nor ever lost an English gun ;
This is he that far away
Against the myriads of Assaye
Clash'd with his fiery few and won ;   100
And underneath another sun,
Warring on a later day,
Round affrighted Lisbon drew
The treble works, the vast designs
Of his labor'd rampart-lines,
Where he greatly stood at bay,
Whence he issued forth anew,
And ever great and greater grew,

Beating from the wasted vines
Back to France her banded swarms,   110
Back to France with countless blows,
Till o'er the hills her eagles flew
Past the Pyrenean pines,
Follow'd up in valley and glen
With blare of bugle, clamor of men,
Roll of cannon and clash of arms,
And England pouring on her foes.
Such a war had such a close.
Again their ravening eagle rose
In anger, wheel'd on Europe-shadowing wings,   120
And barking for the thrones of kings;
Till one that sought but Duty's iron crown
On that loud Sabbath shook the spoiler down;
A day of onsets of despair!
Dash'd on every rocky square
Their surging charges foam'd themselves away;
Last, the Prussian trumpet blew;
Thro' the long-tormented air
Heaven flash'd a sudden jubilant ray.
And down we swept and charged and overthrew.   130
So great a soldier taught us there,
What long-enduring hearts could do.
In that world-earthquake, Waterloo!
Mighty Seaman, tender and true,
And pure as he from taint of craven guile,
O saviour of the silver-coasted isle,
O shaker of the Baltic and the Nile,
If aught of things that here befall
Touch a spirit among things divine,
If love of country move thee there at all,   140
Be glad, because his bones are laid by thine!
And thro' the centuries let a people's voice
In full acclaim,

A people's voice,
The proof and echo of all human fame,
A people's voice, when they rejoice
At civic revel and pomp and game,
Attest their great commander's claim
With honor, honor, honor, honor to him,
Eternal honor to his name.   150

VII.

A people's voice ! we are a people yet.
Tho' all men else their nobler dreams forget
Confused by brainless mobs and lawless Powers ;
Thank Him who isled us here, and roughly set
His Briton in blown seas and storming showers,
We have a voice, with which to pay the debt
Of boundless love and reverence and regret
To those great men who fought, and kept it ours.
And keep it ours, O God, from brute control ;
O Statesmen, guard us, guard the eye, the soul   160
Of Europe, keep our noble England whole,
And save the one true seed of freedom sown
Betwixt a people and their ancient throne,
That sober freedom out of which there springs
Our loyal passion for our temperate kings ;
For, saving that, ye help to save mankind
Till public wrong be crumbled into dust,
And drill the raw world for the march of mind,
Till crowds at length be sane and crowns be just.
But wink no more in slothful overtrust.   170
Remember him who led your hosts ;
He bade you guard the sacred coasts.
Your cannons moulder on the seaward wall ;
His voice is silent in your council-hall
Forever ; and whatever tempests lower
Forever silent ; even if they broke
In thunder, silent ; yet remember all

He spoke among you, and the Man who spoke ;
Who never sold the truth to serve the hour,
Nor palter'd with Eternal God for power ;   180
Who let the turbid streams of rumor flow
Thro' either babbling world of high and low ;
Whose life was work, whose language rife
With rugged maxims hewn from life ;
Who never spoke against a foe ;
Whose eighty winters freeze with one rebuke
All great self-seekers trampling on the right.
Truth-teller was our England's Alfred named ;
Truth-lover was our English Duke :
Whatever record leap to light   190
He never shall be shamed.

VIII.

Lo, the leader in these glorious wars
Now to glorious burial slowly borne,
Follow'd by the brave of other lands,
He, on whom from both her open hands
Lavish Honor shower'd all her stars,
And affluent Fortune emptied all her horn.
Yea, let all good things await
Him who cares not to be great,
But as he saves or serves the state.   200
Not once or twice in our rough island-story,
The path of duty was the way to glory :
He that walks it, only thirsting
For the right, and learns to deaden
Love of self, before his journey closes,
He shall find the stubborn thistle bursting
Into glossy purples, which out-redden
All voluptuous garden-roses.
Not once or twice in our fair island-story,
The path of duty was the way to glory :   210
He, that ever following her commands,

On with toil of heart and knees and hands,
Thro' the long gorge to the far light has won
His path upward, and prevail'd,
Shall find the toppling crags of Duty scaled
Are close upon the shining table-lands
To which our God Himself is moon and sun.
Such was he : his work is done.
But while the races of mankind endure,
Let his great example stand   220
Colossal, seen of every land,
And keep the soldier firm, the statesman pure ;
Till in all lands and' thro' all human story
The path of duty be the way to glory :
And let the land whose hearths he saved from shame
For many and many an age proclaim
At civic revel and pomp and game,
And when the long-illumined cities flame,
Their ever-loyal iron leader's fame,
With honor, honor, honor, honor to him,   230
Eternal honor to his name.

IX.

Peace, his triumph will be sung
By some yet unmoulded tongue
Far on in summers that we shall not see.
Peace, it is a day of pain
For one about whose patriarchal knee
Late the little children clung :
O peace, it is a day of pain
For one upon whose hand and heart and brain
Once the weight and fate of Europe hung.   240
Ours the pain, be his the gain !
More than is of man's degree
Must be with us, watching here
At this, our great solemnity.
Whom we see not we revere ;

We revere, and we refrain
From talk of battles loud and vain,
And brawling memories all too free
For such a wise humility
As befits a solemn fane :
We revere, and while we hear
The tides of Music's golden sea
Setting toward eternity,
Uplifted high in heart and hope are we,
Until we doubt not that for one so true
There must be other nobler work to do
Than when he fought at Waterloó,
And Victor he must ever be.
For tho' the Giant Ages heave the hill
And break the shore, and evermore
Make and break, and work their will ;
Tho' world on world in myriad myriads roll
Round us, each with different powers,
And other forms of life than ours,
What know we greater than the soul?
On God and Godlike men we build our trust.
Hush, the Dead March wails in the people's ears :
The dark crowd moves, and there are sobs and tears :
The black earth yawns : the mortal disappears ;
Ashes to ashes, dust to dust ;
He is gone who seem'd so great. —
Gone ; but nothing can bereave him
Of the force he made his own
Being here, and we believe him
Something far advanced in state,
And that he wears a truer crown
Than any wreath that man can weave him.
But speak no more of his renown,
Lay your earthly fancies down,
And in the vast cathedral leave him.
God accept him, Christ receive him.

NOTES.

ABBREVIATIONS USED IN THE NOTES.

Bayne, Mr. Peter Bayne's *Lessons from My Masters* (Amer. ed., 1879).

Brimley, Mr. George Brimley's paper on Tennyson in *Cambridge Essays*, 1855.

Carr, Mr. J. Comyns Carr's papers on Tennyson in *Cornhill Magazine*, Feb. and July, 1880.

Cf. (*confer*), compare.

Corson, Prof. H. Corson's ed. of Tennyson's *Dream of Fair Women and Two Voices* (New York, 1882).

F. Q., Spenser's *Faërie Queene*.

Fol., following.

Forman, Mr. H. B. Forman's *Our Living Poets* (London, 1871).

Id. (*idem*), the same.

Imp. Dict., Ogilvie's *Imperial Dictionary* (Century Co.'s ed., New York, 1883).

In Mem., Tennyson's *In Memoriam*.

P. L, Milton's *Paradise Lost*.

Prol., prologue.

Shepherd, Mr. R. H. Shepherd's *Tennysoniana* (2d ed., London, 1879).

Stedman, Mr. E. C. Stedman's *Victorian Poets* (Boston, 1876).

Tainsh, Mr. E. C. Tainsh's *Study of the Works of Alfred Tennyson* (London, 1868).

Wace, Mr. W. E. Wace's *Alfred Tennyson, His Life and Works* (Edinburgh, 1881).

Warren, Hon. J. L. Warren's "Bibliography of Tennyson," in *Fortnightly Review*, Oct. 1, 1865.

Wb., Webster's Dictionary (revised quarto ed. of 1879).

Worc., Worcester's Dictionary (quarto ed.).

The abbreviations of the names of Shakespeare's plays will be readily understood. The line-numbers are those of the "Globe" edition.

NOTE. — Tennyson was born August 9th, 1809. In the spring of 1827 the *Poems by Two Brothers* (Alfred and his elder brother Charles) was published. In 1829 Arthur Hallam and Tennyson competed at Cambridge for the Chancellor's gold medal for a poem on *Timbuctoo*; and Tennyson's poem, which won the prize, was published the same year. In 1830 appeared the first volume to which Tennyson affixed his name, *Poems, chiefly Lyrical*; and in the winter of 1832, a second volume of *Poems*. After an almost unbroken silence of ten years, the poet published in 1842 a two-volume edition of his *Poems*, including selections from the earlier volumes (long out of print) and many new pieces. As will be seen by our Notes, nearly all the poems in the present selection appeared in the editions of 1830, 1832, and 1842; and of the more recent publications of the poet it is hardly necessary to say anything here.

NOTES.

" The good Haroun Alraschid."

RECOLLECTIONS OF THE ARABIAN NIGHTS.

THE poem first appeared in the *Poems chiefly Lyrical*, published in
30.
Tainsh remarks that it is " interesting as foreshadowing the power of

detailed description, vivid and very pictorial, which shows itself fully in the *Palace of Art.*"

Bayne speaks of it as a piece " which decisively announced the rise of a great poet." He adds : " The linguistic opulence of the poem is a small matter compared with the imagination required to plan and the fancy to execute such a work. The whole is a thing of the mind, a vision founded upon no fact, and yet we accompany the poet in his voyage down the Tigris with as distinct a realization of his where-abouts as if he were detailing the stages of a journey between Oxford and Twickenham. We see the blaze of light falling in golden green upon the leaves, when suddenly the million tapers of the Caliphate illu-minate the scene ; and we, as well as the poet, are drawn on in wonder-ing curiosity until we are in the presence of the monarch."

2. *Silken sail.* Cf. *Lady of Shalott,* 22 : " The shallop flitteth silken-sail'd," etc.

5. *Sheeny.* Cf. *Madeline :* " Hues of the silken sheeny woof ; " and *Love and Death :* " Love wept and spread his sheeny vans for flight." We find *sheen* as an adjective in Spenser, *F. Q.* ii. 1. 10 : " so faire and sheene."

6. *Adown.* Used both as preposition and as adverb. Cf. 30 below ; and see also *Lotos-Eaters,* 19, 76, etc.

12. *Anight.* By night ; as in Shakespeare, *A. Y. L.* ii. 4. 48 : " Com-ing anight to Jane Smile ; " and Chaucer, *Legende of Goode Women,* 1473 : " With tempest thider were yblow anyghte."

13. *Drove.* Drove over ; a rare use of the verb. For *bloomed,* cf. Hakluyt, *Voyages :* " full of wild corne and peason bloomed, as thick, as ranke, and as faire as any can be seene in Britaine."

23. *Platans.* Plane-trees (Latin *platanus*) ; as in *Princess,* iii. 159 : " the thick-leaved platans of the vale."

47. *Rivage.* Bank. Cf. Spenser, *F. Q.* iv. 6. 20 :

> " The which Pactolus with his waters shere
> Throws forth upon the rivage round about him nere."

48. *Rillets.* A diminutive, like *rivulet, streamlet,* etc.

58. *Engrain'd.* Dyed, colored. Cf. Spenser, *Shep. Kal.* Feb. : " With leaves engrained in lusty greene," etc.

59. *Marge.* Cf. *Morte d'Arthur,* 116 : " about the marge," etc.

64. *Tiars.* A contraction of *tiaras.*

68. *Coverture.* Cf. Shakespeare, *Much Ado,* iii. 1. 30 : " the woodbine coverture."

70. *Bulbul.* The Persian name of the nightingale. Cf. *Princess,* iv. 103 :

> " but smiling, ' Not for thee,' she said,
> ' O Bulbul, any rose of Gulistan
> Shall burst her veil,' " etc.

71. *Not he ; but something,* etc. Cf. Shelley, *To a Skylark :*

> " Hail to thee, blithe Spirit !
> *Bird thou never wert,*
> That from heaven, or near it,
> Pourest thy full heart
> In profuse strains of unpremeditated art."

84. *Counterchanged.* Variegated. Cf. *In Mem.* 89:

> " Witch-elms that counterchange the floor
> Of this flat lawn with dusk and bright."

101. *Pleasance.* Pleasure. Cf. *Lilian:* " Pleasance in love-sighs ; " Spenser, *F. Q.* i. 2. 30: "Faire seemely pleasaunce each to other makes," etc.

103. *Stilly sound.* Cf. " dully sound " in *Palace of Art,* 275.

106. *Rosaries.* Gardens or beds of roses ; the etymological meaning of the word (Latin *rosarium*).

115. *Cedarn.* Cf. *Geraint and Enid:* " A cedarn cabinet." See also Milton, *Comus,* 990 : " About the cedarn alleys."

125. *Silvers.* That is, silver candlesticks ; perhaps a unique instance of the plural.

127. *Mooned.* Crowned with the Mohammedan crescent.

135. *Argent-lidded.* Cf. *Dream of Fair Women,* 158: " The polish'd argent of her breast ; " and *St. Agnes,* 16: " To yonder argent round."

148. *Diaper'd.* Entirely covered, as in diaper work.

THE POET.

THIS poem also appeared in the 1830 volume. The *Westminster Review,* of Jan. 1831, referred to it as giving the author's " own just conception of the grandeur of a poet's destiny." The passage closes prophetically thus : " If our estimate of Mr. Tennyson be correct, he too is a poet ; and many years hence may he read his juvenile description of that character with the proud consciousness that it has become the description and history of his own work."

3. *Dower'd with the hate of hate,* etc. Of course this means that the poet hates hate, etc. It is curious that F. W. Robertson should have explained it thus : " That is, the Prophet of Truth receives for his dower the scorn of men in whose breasts scorn dwells, hatred from men who hate, while his reward is in the gratitude and affection of men who seek the truth which they love, more eagerly than the faults which their acuteness can blame." His comment on the next stanza, in connection with which he quotes lines 33–40 below, is better : " Rare gifts of nature : power to read the ' open secret of the universe ; ' the apostleship of light, truth, liberty ; the faculty of discerning the life and meaning which underlie all forms : this is Tennyson's notion of a poet."

15. *From Calpe unto Caucasus. Calpe,* one of the Pillars of Hercules, was a limit of the ancient world to the west, as *Caucasus* was to the east.

19. *The field-flower.* The dandelion, for instance.

25. *Bravely.* In the old sense of admirably ; as in Shakespeare,

Temp. v. 1. 241, where in reply to Ariel's question, " Was 't well done ? " Prospero says, " Bravely, my diligence ! "   Cf. also *Cymb.* ii. 2. 15 :

> " How bravely thou becom'st thy bed, fresh lily,
> And whiter than the sheets ! "

35. *The wreaths of floating dark upcurl'd.*   The breaking up of the darkness like mist or cloud.

THE LADY OF SHALOTT.

THE poem (first published in 1832) is founded upon the Arthurian legend which was later made the subject of *Lancelot and Elaine.*
5. *Camelot.*   The capital of Arthur.   Cf. *Gareth and Lynette :*

> " Camelot, a city of shadowy palaces
> And stately, rich in emblem and the work
> Of ancient kings who did their days in stone ;
> Which Merlin's hand, the Mage of Arthur's court,
> Knowing all arts, had touch'd, and everywhere
> At Arthur's ordinance, tipt with lessening peak
> And pinnacle, and had made it spire to heaven."

10. *Willows whiten*, etc.   The first reading was :

> " Willows whiten, aspens shiver,
> The sunbeam showers break and quiver
> In the stream that runneth ever," etc.

11. *Dusk and shiver.*   No words could better express the effect of the breezes on the water.
30. *Cheerly.*   Cheerily, cheerfully.   Cf. Shakespeare, *Rich. II.* i. 3. 66 : " But lusty, young, and cheerly drawing breath," etc.
71. *I am half sick of shadows.*   The exclamation is most significant and pathetic.
83. *Like to some branch of stars*, etc.   Tennyson abounds in astronomical figures and allusions.   Cf. the next stanza.
87. *Baldric.*   Belt ; used by Tennyson only here, as by Shakespeare only in *Much Ado*, i. 1. 244 : " hang my bugle in an invisible baldric."
101. *Hooves.*   The old plural of *hoof*, used by the poet nowhere else, though we find *white-hoov'd* in *Œnone*, 50.
157. *Dead-pale between.*   The reading down to 1873 was " A corse between," etc.

THE MILLER'S DAUGHTER.

THIS poem has undergone many changes since its first appearance in the volume of 1832.   There it began with the following stanza, the loss of which no one will much regret :

> " I met in all the close green ways,
>   While walking with my line and rod,
> The wealthy miller's mealy face,
>   Like the moon in an ivy-tod.
> He look'd so jolly and so good,
>   While fishing in the mill-dam water,
> I laugh'd to see him as he stood,
>   And dreamt not of the miller's daughter."

The second stanza, now the first, remains unaltered; and the only change in the next is *can make* for " makes " in the last line.

18. *Own sweet.* The original version has " darling " here, and " own sweet " for *darling* in 23.

20. *Shall be unriddled.* Cf. *The Two Voices,* 170 : " the riddle of the earth ; " and *Palace of Art,* 213 : " the riddle of the painful earth."

33. *Long and listless.* Note the alliteration with *l* in this stanza, as also in the 10th and 11th below.

42. *Making moan.* Cf. *Princess,* vii. 206 : " the moan of doves in immemorial elms ; " and see our ed. p. 185.

52. *Glance and poise.* " If you looked at minnows every day for a week, you would not learn much more about them than lies in these two words. The whole biography of a minnow is there. To poise in perfect stillness and almost perfect invisibility, and then to become visible for the tenth part of a second in that strange glancing gleam, or glint, of the silvery side, as the tiny creature darts away — this is the complete circle of a minnow's observable activities " (Bayne).

53. *When.* Some editions have " where."

59. (*'Twas April then*), etc. The early reading is :

> " ('T was April then) I came and lay
>   Beneath those gummy chestnut buds
>   That glisten'd in the April blue."

" *Breezy blue,* though an after-thought, describes an April day almost by inspiration. Nothing can be truer to nature than the suppressed '*gummy* chestnut buds,' but the word is ugly and would offend weak-stomached Tennysonian brethren "* (Warren).

67. *In my head.* All the earlier eds. have " in the head."
The stanza well describes what most readers will recognize as a familiar experience.

73. *A trout.* In the first version

> " a water-rat from off the bank
> Plung'd in the stream."

76. *And there a vision,* etc. The early reading is :

> " Down looking thro' the sedges rank
>   I saw your troubled image there.
> Upon the dark and dimpled beck
>   It wander'd like a floating light."

93. *My mother thought,* etc. As Bayne remarks, this shows " a curious maturity of observation " in a writer of twenty-two. " A piece of

---

* As it did Christopher North. See *Blackwood,* May, 1832.

knowledge this which one would expect to be more clearly apprehended by an old man than a stripling. Often, indeed, as life goes on, and as we live over again in meditation the scenes of by-gone years, our own actions and the feelings and motives of other people, which were dim to us at the time, become distinct. Experience has taught us to interpret. In exquisite dramatic accordance, also, with the retrospective interest of an elderly man, is the specification of objects which happy love clothed, for him, with a new charm. Had you asked the youth, he would have spoken only of his Alice ; the old man dwells garrulously, and with Morland-like picturesqueness of detail, on the objects which had been gilded with the light of love." [Bayne then quotes the next stanza : " I loved the brimming wave," etc.]

97. *I loved*, etc. The first quatrain of the stanza was originally as follows :

> " How dear to me in youth, my love,
>   Was everything about the mill —
> The black and silent pool above,
>   The pool beneath that ne'er stood still," etc.

98. *Meadows round the mill.* Alliteration with *m* runs through the stanza. See on 33 above.

105. *And oft in ramblings*, etc. The early reading was thus :

> " In rambling on the eastern wold,
>   When thro' the showery April nights
> Their hueless crescent glimmer'd cold,
>   From all the other village lights
> I knew your taper far away.
>   My heart was full of trembling hope,
> Down from the wold I came and lay
>   Upon the dewy swarded slope."

The following stanza, now suppressed, preceded the above :

> " That slope beneath the chestnut tall,
>   Is woo'd with choicest breaths of air :
> Methinks that I could tell you all
>   The cowslips and the king-cups there ;
> Each coltsfoot down the grassy bent,
>   Whose round leaves hold the gather'd shower,
> Each quaintly-folded cuckoo pint,
>   Each silver-paly cuckoo flower."

117. *O that I were*, etc. The following has also been suppressed :

> " O that I were the wreath she wreathes,
>   The mirror where her sight she feeds,
> The song she sings, the air she breathes,
>   The letters of the book she reads."

129. *But when at last*, etc. The first version was as follows :

> " I loved, but when I dared to speak
>   My love, the lanes were white with may ;
> Your ripe lips moved not, but your cheek
>   Flush'd like the coming of the day.
> Rose-cheekt, rose-lipt, half-sly, half-shy,
>   You would, and would not, little one,
> Although I pleaded tenderly,
>   And you and I were all alone."

130. *With may.* That is, with the white hawthorn blossoms; not "with May," as sometimes misprinted. Cf. *Guinevere*, 22 : "Green-suited, but with plumes that mock'd the may." But in *The Coming of Arthur*, we find "white with May," the reference being to the flowers of the month in general, as the context shows :

> "Far shone the fields of May thro' open door,
> The sacred altar blossom'd white with May,
> The sun of May descended on their king ; "

and again : " Blow trumpet, for the world is white with May."

137. *And slowly was my mother brought*, etc. The bringing of his betrothed to visit his mother does not appear in the first version, but was added in 1842, the following stanzas being omitted to make room for the three new ones :

> " Remember you the clear moonlight
>   That whiten'd all the eastern ridge,
> When o'er the water, dancing white,
>   I stepp'd upon the old mill-bridge?
> I heard you whisper from above
>   A lute-toned whisper, ' I am here ; '
> I murmur'd, ' Speak again, my love,
>   The stream is loud ; I cannot hear.'
>
> " I heard, as I have seem'd to hear,
>   When all the under air was still,
> The low voice of the glad new year
>   Call to the freshly-flower'd hill.
> I heard, as I have often heard
>   The nightingale in leafy woods
> Call to its mate, when nothing stirr'd
>   To left or right but falling floods."

Bayne remarks : " The young squire marries the miller's daughter. All the traditions of worldliness, all the rules of Mammon-worship, all those buckram proprieties which are woven into shrouds and cerements to crush the soul out of living men and women, are defied in such an arrangement. Had the boy-squire's father been alive, it might not have been practicable. In no instance does Tennyson make the father bend his pride to consent to the unequal marriage of a son or of a daughter. But, like Chaucer, Shakespeare, and Ruskin, he seems to have lurking somewhere in his heart a faith that women, when they *are* good, are infinitely good, infallibly wise, capable of getting nearer to the mother-heart of nature than men. The squire, had he been alive, might have made insuperable difficulties, but the mother did what was right."

203. *Love, that hath*, etc. This song was substituted in 1842 for one beginning " All yesternight you met me not."

221. *A many.* This expression is obsolete, though we still say *a few*, and *many a* in a distributive sense. Cf. Shakespeare, *K. John*, iv. 2. 199: " Told of a many thousand warlike French ; " *M. of V.* iii. 5. 73: " A many fools," etc.

223. *Yet tears they shed*, etc. This stanza and the next were added in 1842.

229. *Had brought.* The reading of the English ed. of 1884. All the American eds. we have seen (from 1849 down) read " that brought."

239. *Arise, and let us wander forth*, etc.   The original reading is:

> "I've half a mind to walk, my love,
> To the old mill across the wolds,
> For look! the sunset from above
> Winds all the vale in rosy folds," etc.

ŒNONE.

FIRST printed in the 1832 volume, but considerably altered since.

4. *Puts forth an arm*, etc.   One must have watched the mists floating through a wooded valley, to appreciate the accuracy of this description. Cf. 90 below.

11. *Stands up and takes the morning.*   There is a Dorian simplicity and vigor in this picture of the mountain-top catching the first flush of the dawn.

15. *Forlorn of.*   Bereft of.   For the participial, use, cf. Chaucer, *Franklin's Tale:* "Aurelius, that his cost hath al forlorn" (lost); etc. We find the past tense in Spenser, *F. Q.* iii. 9. 52: "In her fraile witt, that now her quite forlore" (deserted), etc.

19. *A fragment.*   That is, a broken rock.   The use of the word is somewhat peculiar.   In 218 below the *tumbled from the glens* makes it clear what the *fragments* are; but *twined with vine* gives us no such information.

22. *O mother Ida*, etc.   Stedman, commenting on Tennyson's indebtedness to Theocritus, remarks: "It is in the *Œnone* that we discover Tennyson's earliest adaptation of that *refrain* which was a striking beauty of the pastoral elegiac verse.   'O mother Ida, hearken ere I die' is the analogue of (Theocr. ii.) 'See thou, whence came my love, O lady Moon;' of the refrain to the lament of Daphnis (Theocr. i.), 'Begin, dear Muse, begin the woodland song;' and of the recurrent wail in the *Epitaph of Bion* (Mosch. iii.), 'Begin, Sicilian Muses, begin the song of your sorrow!'   Throughout the poem the Syracusan manner and feeling are strictly and nobly maintained."

24. *For now the noonday quiet*, etc.   Stedman compares and translates the *Thalysia* (Theocr. vii.):

> "Whither at noonday dost thou drag thy feet?
> For now the lizard sleeps upon the wall,
> The crested lark is wandering no more" —

and *The Enchantress* (Theocr. ii.):

> "Lo, now the sea is silent, and the winds
> Are hush'd.   Not silent is the wretchedness
> Within my breast; but I am all aflame
> With love for him who made me thus forlorn, —
> A thing of evil, neither maid nor wife."

Mr. J. C. Carr (*Cornhill Mag.* Jan. 1880) notes that the first line is literally translated from Callimachus, *Lavacrum Palladis:* μεσαμβρινὰ δ'εἶχ' ὄρος ἀσυχία.

27. *And the winds are dead.* All the eds. we have seen (including that of 1873) down to 1884 have " and the cicala sleeps ; " and in the next line, " flowers droop." It probably occurred to the poet that the introduction of the *cicala*, or cicada (the *Greek* cicada, not our insect so called), was too nearly a repetition of that of the *grasshopper.*

30. *My eyes are full of tears,* etc. Cf. Shakespeare, 2 *Hen. VI.* ii. 3. 17 : " Mine eyes are full of tears, my heart of grief."

39. *As yonder walls,* etc. According to Ovid (*Heroides,* xv. 179), Troy owed its origin to the music of Apollo's lyre. Cf. *Tithonus :*

> " Like that strange song I heard Apollo sing
> While Ilion like a mist rose into towers ; "

and *Princess,* iii. 326:

> "the crowned towers
> Built to the Sun."

50. *White-hoov'd.* See on *Lady of Shalott,* 101 above.

51. *Simois.* A small river in Troas, flowing into the Scamander. Cf. 202 below.

65. *Of pure Hesperian gold.* From the gardens of the Hesperides.

74. *Married brows.* Meeting eyebrows.

82. *Delivering.* Announcing; as in Shakespeare, *Rich. II.* iii. 3. 34 :

> " Through brazen trumpet send the breath of parle
> Into his ruin'd ears, and thus deliver," etc.

94. *Brake.* The poet uses both *brake* and *broke.* See *Princess,* p. 149.

102. *Peacock.* The bird was sacred to Here, or Juno. Cf. Shakespeare, *Temp.* iv. 1. 74: " her peacocks fly amain," etc.

113. *Mine.* The early reading is " mines."

129. *Rest in a happy place,* etc. Cf. *Lotos-Eaters,* 156 :

> " For they lie beside their nectar, and the bolts are hurl'd
> Far below them in the valleys, and the clouds are lightly curl'd
> Round their golden houses," etc.

See also Virgil, *Æn.* iv. 379 :

> " Scilicet is Superis labor est, ea cura quietos
> Solicitat ! "

137. *O'erthwarted with the brazen-headed spear.* That is, with the spear athwart or across them.

151. *Sequel of guerdon.* Addition of prize or honorary tribute.

161. *Until endurance,* etc. The first version reads thus :

> " so endurance,
> Like to an athlete's arm, shall still become
> Sinew'd with motion, till thine active will
> (As the dark body of the Sun robed round
> With his own ever-emanating lights)
> Be flooded o'er with her own effluences,
> And thereby grow to freedom."

170. *Idalian.* Aphrodite or Venus was so called from *Idalium,* a mountain-city in Cyprus, which, like Paphos, was one of her favorite seats.

174. *Lucid.* Cf. *Princess,* ii. 10: "lucid marbles," etc.

178. *Sunlights.* Spots of sunshine, the "tremulous isles of light" of *The Princess,* vi. 65. See our ed. p. 180.

192. *Fairest — why fairest wife?* etc. Stedman compares Theocr. **xx.**:

> "O shepherds, tell me truth! Am I not fair?
> Hath some god made me, then, from what I was,
> Off-hand, another being? . . .
> Along the mountains all the women call
> Me beautiful, all love me."

197. *Most loving is she?* Bayne says : "Œnone wails melodiously for Paris without the remotest suggestion of fierceness or revengeful wrath. She does not upbraid him for having preferred to her the fairest and most loving wife in Greece, but wonders how any one could love him better than she does. A Greek poet would have used his whole power of expression to instil bitterness into her resentful words. The classic legend, instead of representing Œnone as forgiving Paris, makes her nurse her wrath throughout all the anguish and terror of the Trojan War. At its end, her Paris comes back to her. Deprived of Helen, a broken and baffled man, he returns from the smoking ruins of his native Troy, and entreats Œnone to heal him of a wound, which, unless she lends her aid, must be mortal. Œnone gnashes her teeth at him, refuses him the remedy, and lets him die. In the end, no doubt, she falls into remorse, and kills herself — this is quite in the spirit of classic legend; implacable vengeance, soul-sickened with its own victory, dies in despair. That forgiveness of injuries could be anything but weakness — that it could be honorable, beautiful, brave — is an entirely Christian idea ; and it is because this idea, although it has not yet practically conquered the world, although it has indeed but slightly modified the conduct of nations, has nevertheless secured recognition as ethically and socially right, that Tennyson could not hope to enlist the sympathy and admiration of his readers for his Œnone, if he had cast her image in the tearless bronze of Pagan obduracy."

220. *The Abominable.* Eris, the goddess of Discord.

249. *A shudder comes,* etc. This touch was added in the 1842 edition.

259. *Cassandra.* The prophetic daughter of Priam.

264. *All earth and air,* etc. Mr. J. C. Carr (*Cornhill Mag.* Jan. 1880) compares Webster, *Duchess of Malfi,* iv. 2 :

> "The heaven o'er my head seems made of molten brass,
> The earth of flaming sulphur."

THE PALACE OF ART.

THIS is another of the poems in the volume of 1832 which has been much altered from the original version. Warren says : "Here, more than elsewhere, we regret the omission of so many exquisite verses that we have no space to quote all. The following is, however, so interesting that we must give it, note included:

"'When I first conceived the plan of the Palace of Art, I intended to have introduced both sculptures and paintings into it; but it is the most difficult of all things to *devise* a statue in verse. Judge whether I have succeeded in the statues of Elijah and Olympias:

> One was the Tishbite whom the raven fed,
>   As when he stood on Carmel-steeps
> With one arm stretch'd out bare, and mock'd and said,
>   "Come, cry aloud — he sleeps!"
>
> Tall, eager, lean, and strong, his cloak wind-borne
>   Behind, his forehead heavenly-bright
> From the clear marble pouring glorious scorn,
>   Lit as with inner light.
>
> One was Olympias: the floating snake
>   Roll'd round her ankles, round her waist
> Knotted, and folded once about her neck
>   Her perfect lips to taste:
>
> Round by the shoulder moved: she seeming blithe
>   Declined her head: on every side
> The dragon's curves melted and mingled with
>   The woman's youthful pride
>
> Of rounded limbs.'

"Certainly no one but their author could have been in doubt about the success of these stanzas. If, indeed, Elijah be more of a picture than a statue, Olympias is as clear and calm as the Fates of the Elgin Marbles. The power of wedding intense passion with as intense a majesty of repose is the true master's mark.

"The stanzas next to be quoted are not less successful in a direction comparatively new to poetry. The poet's love of astronomy, the results of which culminate in this superb passage, have besides led to the naturalization through him into modern English poetry of numberless astronomic terms and metaphors. Any one versed in the Laureate's poetry can supply ample illustrations for himself; but, if he has never read the following lines, they will open richer worlds to him. They are 'expressive of the joy wherewith the soul contemplated the results of astronomical experiment:' —

> Hither, when all the deep unsounded skies
>   Shuddered with silent stars, she clomb,
> And as with optic glasses her keen eyes
>   Pierced through the mystic dome,
>
> Regions of lucid matter taking forms,
>   Brushes of fire, hazy gleams,
> Clusters and beds of worlds, and bee-like swarms
>   Of suns, and starry streams.
>
> She saw the snowy poles of moonless Mars,
>   That marvellous round of milky light
> Below Orion, and those double stars
>   Whereof the one more bright
>
> Is circled by the other, etc.

"We must conclude our extracts with one charming little picture, hoping only that the grandeur of the preceding verses may not spoil its comparatively sober effect :

> Or blue-eyed Kriemhilt from a craggy hold,
> Athwart the light-green rows of vine,
> Pour'd blazing hoards of Nibelungen gold,
> Down to the gulfy Rhine."

The Palace of Art, as Bayne remarks, " is one of many poems in which Tennyson becomes the ethical instructor as well as the poetical entertainer of his age. The truth he expounds and inculcates is very old, very simple, but of infinite importance, and specially requiring enforcement in a time of ripe intellectual civilization, and of the fastidiousness, cynicism, and cultured pride which are its besetting sins. Avoiding, with a willingness to make himself intelligible and useful which I wish he had exhibited in some other instances, the risk of being treated as having many meanings or none, he states, in a few lines addressed to an unnamed friend, his purpose in the poem. It is an allegory of a soul possessed of many gifts, loving beauty and knowledge, and even good in so far as goodness may gratify an æsthetic taste, but forgetting that beauty, knowledge, and goodness ought to be made vassals unto charity :

> And he that shuts love out, in turn shall be
> Shut out from Love, and on her threshold lie
> Howling in outer darkness.

The palace of art is ' a lordly pleasure-house,' built by the poet for his soul, in which all the delights of intellect and imagination — all the charm of fancied superiority to the mass of men — combine to make her happy. The problem to be solved is whether man *can* thus be made nobly and permanently happy, and the solution is experimental; that is to say, the poet places imaginatively before us a soul in the enjoyment of all delights, save spiritual and moral, realizes her experience step by step, and finds, in the concluding stage of that experience, the solution of which he is in quest. . . .

"The essence of the sin was not culture, but the selfishness and aristocraticism of cultured pride; not delight, whether of the senses or of the mind, but delight unshared by others; not abstention from the partisanship of creeds, but contemptuous isolation from those who accept them, and lack of sympathetic appreciation of the truth they contain. Such isolation, such pride, such culture, are indeed damnable."

6. *I chose,* etc. The early reading was "I chose, whose ranged ramparts ;" and in the next line, "great broad " for *level.*

15. *While Saturn whirls,* etc. The shadow of the planet, projected on the ring, is a striking feature of the Saturnian system, as seen in the telescope.

30. *That lent broad verge.* That gave a broad horizon. For *verge* in this sense, cf. *Princess,* iv. 29: "That sinks with all we love below the verge ;" *Id.* vii. 23: "the slope of sea from verge to shore ;" and *The Gardener's Daughter:* "and May from verge to verge."

49. *Traced.* Ornamented with tracery ; a rare use of the word.

61. *Arras.* Tapestry. The description of the designs which follows

is the utmost perfection of word-painting. Each stanza is a finished picture.

80. *And hoary to the wind.* To appreciate this touch, one must have seen a grove of olive-trees when the peculiar whitish-gray underside of the leaves is turned up by the wind.

81. *And one a foreground,* etc. What an amount of detail in the four lines, which bring before the eye with almost the painter's power the triple wall of mountains rising from the volcanic plain in the foreground !

83. *The scornful crags.* The epithet is striking, and appropriate enough here ; but the poet did well to suppress a similar use of it in *Œnone —*

> " The golden-sandall'd morn
> Rose-hued the scornful hills " —

as savoring too much of "modern subjectivity" in the description of nature.

96. *Babe in arm.* The reviewers of the volume of 1832 made merry over this phrase, comparing it with the " lance in rest " of the romances of chivalry ; but the poet has not only retained it here but repeated it in the *Princess,* vi. 15 :

> " But high upon the palace Ida stood
> With Psyche's babe in arm."

105. *Uther's deeply wounded son.* That is, King Arthur. Cf. the *Morte d' Arthur,* 306 below.
In the original version this stanza reads thus :

> " And that deep-wounded child of Pendragon
> Mid misty woods on sloping greens
> Dozed in the valley of Avilion
> Tended by crowned queens."

111. *The Ausonian king.* Numa Pompilius, the second King of Rome, who was said to have received his laws from the nymph Egeria. Cf. *Princess,* ii. 65 : "she That taught the Sabine how to rule." In the present passage the original reading was "the Tuscan king."

113. *Engrail'd.* Indented ; an heraldic term.

115. *Cama.* The Hindu god of love, the Indian Cupid, whose name is also given as Kama, Kama-dew, Kama-deva, Camdeo, etc. He is sometimes represented as riding by night on a parrot, or lory ; as in Southey's *Curse of Kehama,* x. 19 :

> " 'T was Camdeo riding on his lory,
> 'T was the immortal youth of love," etc.

See also Sir William Jones's *Hymn to Camdeo :*

> " O thou for ages born, yet ever young,
> For ages may thy Brahmin's lay be sung !
> And when thy lory spreads his emerald wings
> To waft thee high above the towers of kings,
> Whilst o'er thy throne the moon's pale light
> Pours her soft radiance thro' the night," etc.

116. *Or sweet Europa's mantle blew,* etc.   The edition of 1875 has
"blue" for *blew,* but the latter is the reading of the earlier eds. and
also of that of 1884.   We suspect that the printer was responsible for
the change ; but if it was the poet, he has done well in restoring what
he first wrote.

Stedman compares Moschus, ii. 125 fol. :

> "But she, upon the ox-like back of Zeus
> Sitting, with one hand held the bull's great horn,
> And with the other her garment's purple fold
> Drew upward, that the infinite hoary spray
> Of the salt ocean might not drench it through ;
> The while Europa's mantle by the winds
> Was filled and swollen like a vessel's sail,
> Buoying the maiden onward."

121. *Ganymede.*   There is another allusion to the lovely boy carried
off by Jove's eagle, in the *Princess,* iii. 55 :

> "They mounted, Ganymedes,
> To tumble, Vulcans, on the second morn."

137. *The Ionian father,* etc.   Homer.

149. *The people here,* etc.   "Could Count de Montalembert convey, in
any number of volumes, a more accurate account of 'the state of society in France,' before and during the first Revolution, than is contained
in this stanza ? " (Bayne.)

163. *Verulam.*   Bacon.   Cf. *Princess,* ii. 144 : "But Homer, Plato,
Verulam," etc.

164. *The first of those who know.*   As Mr. Carr notes, this is translated from Dante, who calls Aristotle "Il maestro di color che sanno."

171. *Memnon.*   Cf. *Princess,* iii. 100 : "A Memnon smitten with the
rising sun."

174. *Her low preamble.*   Some one has fancifully suggested that the
poet makes the nightingale feminine in *The Princess,* i 218 (" Rapt in
her song "), because the bird is within the grounds of Ida's exclusively
feminine college — just as mine host, a few lines before (i. 187), said
that he "always made a point to post with mares," etc.   In the present
passage, however, we find Tennyson again following (as the poets generally do) ancient fable rather than modern ornithology.   In *The Gardener's Daughter,* on the other hand, he is true to the latter :

> "The redcap whistled ; and the nightingale
> Sang loud, as tho' he were the bird of day."

175. *To hear her echo'd voice,* etc.   Some English critic sneers at this
as an acoustic impossibility ; but the obvious meaning is that she hears
her voice echoing through the vaulted rooms.

186. *Anadems.*   Garlands, chaplets.   Cf. Drayton, *Owle,* 1168 : "Drest
this Tree with Anadems of flowers ; " Shelley, *Adonais :*

> "Another clipt her profuse locks, and threw
> The wreath upon him, like an anadem."

192. *Be flatter'd to the height.*   In the editions down to 1853, this is
followed by these two stanzas, for which the next *three* (as they now
stand) were substituted :

> " ' From shape to shape at first within the womb
>   The brain is modell'd,' she began,
>   ' And thro' all phases of all thought I come
>   Into the perfect man.
>
> " ' All Nature widens upward. Evermore
>   The simpler essence lower lies:
>   More complex is more perfect, owning more
>   Discourse, more widely wise.' "

This is admirable as a statement of a great scientific truth, but the poet may have decided that it was out of place here.

204. *Drives them to the deep.* See *Matt.* viii. 32.

209. *I take possession,* etc. The reading down to 1853 was as follows:

> " I take possession of men's minds and deeds.
>   I live in all things great and small.
>   I sit apart holding no forms of creeds,
>   But contemplating all."

213. *The riddle of the painful earth.* See on *Miller's Daughter,* 20 above.

217. *And so she throve,* etc. The reading down to 1853 was:

> " And intellectual throne
>
> Of full-sphered contemplation. So three years
>   She throve, but on the fourth she fell," etc.

219. *Like Herod,* etc. See *Acts,* xii. 21 fol.

222. *God, before whom,* etc. The expression is borrowed from an essay by Arthur Hallam, entitled " Theodicæa Novissima " (see his *Remains,* p. 363) : " I believe that redemption is universal in so far as it left no obstacle between man and God but man's own will; that indeed is in the power of God's election, with whom alone rest the abysmal secrets of personality."

227. *Wrote ' Mene, mene,'* etc. See *Daniel,* v. 25 fol.

241. *And hollow shades,* etc. Cf. Beckford, *Vathek :* " Soliman raised his hands toward heaven in token of supplication, and the caliph discerned thro' his bosom, which was transparent as crystal, his heart enveloped in flames."

242. *Fretted.* Wrinkled, as in the young babe.

247. *Onward-sloping.* Tennyson is fond of the word *slope,* both noun and verb. He often uses the latter to express motion; as in *Œnone,* 3, 21, *Princess,* iii. 273, vii. 197, *Locksley Hall,* 8, *Geraint and Enid,* 76, etc.

251. *The plunging seas.* No word could better express the sound than *plunging.* Cf. *Dream of Fair Women,* 118 below.

255. *Circumstance.* The surrounding universe. Cf. *In Mem.* 64 : " And breasts the blows of circumstance ; " where it is used in a similar though more limited sense.

275. *Dully.* Perhaps the poet's own coinage ; not found in Wb. or Worc. Cf. *stilly* in *Arab. Nights,* 103.

282. *Rocks.* The eds. down to 1853 have " stones."

THE LOTOS-EATERS.

THE poem appeared first in 1832, and received some additions in 1842. It is founded of course on the Greek legend of the *Lotophagi*, which Homer uses in the *Odyssey*.

"*The Lotos-Eaters* carries Tennyson's tendency to pure æstheticism to an extreme point. It is picture and music, and nothing more. The writer did not suppose he was writing *Hamlet*, or solving 'the riddle of the painful earth.' Nor must we go to the work with that demand upon it. . . . To attempt to treat it as an allegory, which figures forth the tendency to abandon the battle of life, to retire from a fruitless, ever-renewed struggle — to read it as we should read *The Pilgrim's Progress*, and look out for facts of actual experience which answer to its images, is as monstrous and perverse as it would be to test a proposition of geometry by its rhythm and imagery. A mood of feeling, of course, it represents, and feeling dependent on and directed to distinct objects, — in this latter respect alone differing from music. We may, of course, too, apply the mood of feeling thus depicted to the real events of life, and translate it into the actual language of men under the influence of 'mild-eyed melancholy.' So we might with a sonata of Beethoven's, — but the application is ours, and not the composer's; and if we attempt to limit the composer to our interpretation, rather than give ourselves up to his free inspiration from a purely musical impulse, all we get by it is, generally, a very poor verbal poem instead of a noble work that does not, however, belong to the region of articulate speech " (Brimley).

Stedman, in his chapter on "Tennyson and Theocritus," remarks that this poem is "charged from beginning to end with the effects and very language of the Greek pastoral poets. As in *Œnone*, there is no consecutive imitation of any one idyl; but the work is curiously filled out with passages borrowed here and there, as the growth of the poem recalled them at random to the author's mind."

4. *In the afternoon*, etc. "The Argonauts (Theocr. xiii.) come in the afternoon unto a land of cliffs and thickets and streams; of meadows set with sedge, whence they cut for their couches sharp flowering rush and the low galingale " (Stedman).

8. *A downward smoke.* Cf. the "wreaths of dangling water-smoke " in *Princess*, vii. 198.

11. *Slow-dropping veils*, etc. The poet, in a letter to Mr. S. E. Dawson (see our ed. of *The Princess*, pp. 148, 153, 156, etc.) says : " When I was about twenty or twenty-one I went on a tour to the Pyrenees. Lying among those mountains before a waterfall that comes down one thousand or twelve hundred feet, I sketched it (according to my custom then) in these words :

Slow-dropping veils of thinnest lawn.

When I printed this, a critic informed me that 'lawn was the material used in theatres to imitate a waterfall, and graciously added 'Mr.

T. should not go to the boards of a theatre but to nature herself for his suggestions.' And I *had* gone to nature herself.

"I think it is a moot point whether — if I had known how that effect was produced on the stage — I should have ventured to publish the line."

Bayne remarks: "Whoever has seen a stream in its midsummer slenderness of volume, falling down a front of rock divided into steps or ledges, will admit that no words could possibly surpass these in descriptive precision. The Falling Foss, for example — a small cascade on one of the affluents of the Esk, near Whitby — affords a realization so exact of the 'slow-dropping veil of thinnest lawn,' that it at once, · when I saw it last summer, reminded me of the poem ; nor could an officer of the Geological Survey, writing with purely scientific intent, devise a more literal or a more expressive description."

18. *Woven copse.* Cf. 142 below.

19. *Adown.* Cf. *Arab. Nights*, 6, 30, etc.

23. *Galingale.* An English name for the *Cyperus longus,* which grows in wet meadows. See on 4 above, and on 53 below.

38. *Between the sun and moon.* The sun setting in the west as the moon was rising in the east. Some one explains it as = twilight, or between day and night.

42. *The wandering fields.* Cf. Virgil, *Æn.* vi. 724 : "campi liquentes ;" and *Id.* viii. 695 : "arva Neptunia."

46. *There is sweet music here,* etc. Bayne asks : "What imagery could convey the lulling influence of sweet, faint music more movingly than this ? "

50. *Music, that gentlier,* etc. Stedman compares Moschus, ii. 3 :

> " When Sleep, that sweeter on the eyelids lies
> Than honey, and doth fetter down the eyes
> With gentle bond," etc.

and Theocritus, v. 50 :

> " Here, if you come, your feet shall tread on wool,
> The fleece of lambs, softer than downy sleep."

51. *Tired eyelids upon tired eyes.* All the eds. print " tir'd " in both places, contrary to Tennyson's rule not to use the apostrophe when the verb ends in *e.* Did the poet mean to make *tired* monosyllabic ?

53. *Here are cool mosses,* etc. Stedman compares Theocritus, v. 45 fol. ·

> " Here are the oaks, and here is galingale,
> Here bees are sweetly humming near their hives ;
> Here are twin fountains of cool water ; here
> The birds are prattling on the trees, — the shade
> Is deeper than beyond ; and here the pine
> From overhead casts down to us its cones."

70. *Lo, in the middle of the wood,* etc. "Equally wonderful are those lines in which, as contrasted with the feverish unrest, with the tumultuous wearing activity, of human existence, the deep quietude of nature's operations in the vegetable world is shadowed forth " (Bayne).

72. *With.* By ; as often in the Elizabethan writers. See Abbott's *Shakes. Gr.* § 193.

84. *Hateful is the dark-blue sky*, etc. Stedman compares the passage
with Moschus, v. 4 fol. :

> " When the gray deep has sounded, and the sea
> Climbs up in foam and far the loud waves roar,
> I seek for land and trees, and flee the brine,
> And earth to me is welcome ; the dark wood
> Delights me, where, although the great wind blow,
> The pine-tree sings. An evil life indeed
> The fisherman's, whose vessel is his home,
> The sea his toil, the fish his wandering prey.
> But sweet to me to sleep beneath the plane
> Thick-leaved ; and near me I would love to hear
> The babble of the spring, that murmuring
> Perturbs him not, but is the woodman's joy."

90. *Let us alone*, etc. " Surely the philosophy of sad resignation—
the *cui bono*, don't care, *nil admirari* mood, that wants only to rest —
the morphia-crave of a generation that has made the circuit of science,
art, philosophy, to be told at last by Schopenhauer that life is misery
and the universe a failure — never found more appropriate expression "
(Bayne).

109. *Mild-minded melancholy.* In the *Englishman's Magazine* for August, 1831, there is a sonnet by Tennyson which begins thus :

> " Check every outflash, every ruder sally
> Of thought and speech ; speak low, and give up wholly
> Thy spirit to mild-minded Melancholy,'' etc.

114. *Dear is the memory*, etc. This stanza was added in 1842.

116. *But all hath suffer'd change*, etc. It will be borne in mind that
this is the company of Ulysses on their long voyage homeward from
Troy.

131. *By many wars.* The early eds. have " with many wars."

133. *Moly.* The fabulous herb of magic power, —

> " that moly
> That Hermes once to wise Ulysses gave " (*Comus*, 636).

Stedman compares Theocritus, v. 31 :

> " More sweetly will you sing
> Propt underneath the olive, in these groves.
> Here are cool waters plashing down, and here
> The grasses spring ; and here, too, is a bed
> Of leafage, and the locusts babble here."

135. *Eyelid.* The early eds. have " eyelids."

150. *We have had enough of action*, etc. The remainder of the poem
from this point was added in 1842.

156. *For they lie*, etc. Bayne remarks : " Plagiarism is out of the
question, but Tennyson must, I think, have derived the suggestion of
this passage from the Song of the Fates, repeated by Iphigenia at the
end of the fourth act of Goethe's drama. The gods are therein described as sitting at golden tables in everlasting feast, or striding along
from peak to peak of the mountains, while, up through gorge and chasm,
steams to them, like light clouds of altar-smoke, the breath of strangled
Titans :

Sie aber, sie bleiben
In ewigen Festen
An goldenen Tischen.
Sie schreiten vom Berge
Zu Bergen hinüber :
Aus schlünden der Tiefe
Dampft ihnen der Athem
Erstickter Titanen,
Gleich Opfergerüchen,*
Ein leichtes Gewölke.

There can be no thought of plagiarism, because Tennyson's treatment is entirely his own. His substitution of the toiling races of men for the fallen Titans, as objects of contemplation to the happy gods, adds both to the sense of reality and to the pathos of the lines; but the coincidence seems too close to have been purely accidental. The germ, derived from Goethe, may very well have remained in Tennyson's mind without his recollecting whence it came."
See also on *Œnone*, 128 above.

A DREAM OF FAIR WOMEN.

THE poem, originally published in 1832, was considerably altered in the edition of 1842, and again retouched in the editions of 1845 and 1853. For a single additional change, which we note in the edition of 1884, see on 106 below.

5. *Dan Chaucer.* For the title (Latin *dominus*, through the Old French *dans*) cf. Spenser, *F. Q.* iv. 2. 32 : "Dan Chaucer, well of English undefyled ;" and *Id.* vii. 7. 9 :

> "That old Dan Geffrey (in whose gentle spright,
> The pure well head of Poesie did dwell)," etc.

Note also the sportive use of it in Shakespeare, *L L. L.* iii. 1. 182 : "Dan Cupid," etc.

6. *Those melodious bursts,* etc. "The great literary outburst, as it has been called, of the days of Spenser and Shakespeare" (Stopford Brooke).

21. *And clattering flints,* etc. For the correspondence of sound and sense, Corson compares the famous example in Virgil, *Æn.* viii. 596 : "Quadrupedante putrem sonitu quatit ungula campum."

22. *Sanctuaries.* Whither they had fled for refuge. Cf. *Æn.* ii. 512 fol.

23. *Past.* The English eds. print "pass'd," though elsewhere regularly "past." The original reading was "scream'd." "This, though a small point, illustrates the ripening of a true poet. His mind passes from the turbulent to the quiet, from spasm to repose, from the ornate and florid to the simple " (Warren).

27. *Tortoise.* The *testudo* of ancient warfare, the shell-like covering of overlapped shields held above their heads, with which the compact body of soldiers protected themselves against missiles thrown from the walls when storming a town or fortification. The name was also applied to a movable shed used for the same purpose.

For the translation of a classical term into the vernacular, cf. "northern morn" for *aurora borealis* in *Morte d'Arthur*, 190 (see also *Talking Oak*, 275), and "mother-city" for *metropolis* in *Princess*, i. 111 (so "mother town" in *In Mem.* 98).

33. *Squadrons and squares.* Cf. *Princess*, v. 236:

> "the embattled squares
> And squadrons of the Prince."

43. *Strikes along.* Cf. *In Mem.* 15: "The sunbeam strikes along the world." Mr. J. C. Carr remarks that the present passage "would certainly seem to have been suggested by the *Hymn to Hermes:*

> ὡς δ' ὅποτ' ὠκὺς νόημα διὰ στέρνοιο περήσῃ
> Ἀνέρος . . .
> αἱ δέ τε δινηθῶσιν ἀπ' ὀφθαλμῶν ἀμαρυγαί.

47. *Leaguer'd.* Beleaguered; surrounded with a *leaguer* (cf. *Princess*, vii. 18), or besieging army.

49. *All those sharp fancies.* The stanza aptly describes what most readers will probably be conscious of having experienced when falling to sleep.

53. *At last methought,* etc. As Corson remarks, this reminds us of "the opening lines of the *Inferno;* and the 'old wood' has a like meaning with Dante's 'selva oscura.'"

56. *Shook.* Scintillated, twinkled.

71. *Lush green grasses.* Cf. Shakespeare, *Temp.* ii. 1. 52: "How lush and lusty the grass looks! how green!"

76. *Leading from lawn to lawn.* The poet seems to be fond of alliteration with the liquid *l*. See on *Miller's Daughter*, 33; and cf. *Palace of Art*, 68, etc.

78. *Pour'd back*, etc. Corson quotes Wordsworth, *Intimations of Immortality:*

> "bring back the hour
> Of splendor in the grass, of glory in the flower."

85. *A lady.* Helen; "the Greek woman" of *Œnone*, 257.

92. *In her place.* A touch of the old ballad style.

95. *Many drew swords.* Referring to the Trojan war.

100. *One that stood beside.* Iphigenia, the daughter of Agamemnon, who was doomed to be sacrificed to Diana because her father had killed a stag sacred to the goddess. According to the story, she was not slain, Diana having relented and snatched her away, leaving a hind to be sacrificed in her place.

101. *Averse.* Turned away; as in Milton, *P. L.* viii. 138:

> "with her part averse
> From the sun's beam," etc.

104. *This woman.* That is, Helen.

106. *Which men call'd Aulis,* etc. This line appears first, so far as we are aware, in the ed. of 1884. The former reading was " Which yet to name my spirit loathes and fears."

113. *The high masts,* etc. The stanza originally read thus :

> " The tall masts quiver'd as they lay afloat,
>   The temples and the people and the shore,
> One drew a sharp knife thro' my tender throat
>   Slowly, — and nothing more."

It has been generally supposed that Tennyson was led to change the reading * by the ridicule of Lockhart in the *Quarterly Review* (April, 1833) : " What touching simplicity! What genuine pathos! *He cut my throat — nothing more !* One might indeed ask, *What more she would have.*" Possibly, however, as others have suggested, the alteration was made in order to conform to the classical story. As it now stands, it is not said that Iphigenia's throat *is* cut; we may assume that she is snatched away just as the knife touches it.

However that may be, the critics are divided on the question whether the change is for the better. Bayne says of the original reading : " The picture, as drawn by the poet, is perfectly in keeping with itself, perfectly complete. With a force of dramatic sympathy which it would be quite reasonable to compare with Shakespeare's, Tennyson enters into the person of the girl that is about to die, and enables the imaginative reader to see through her eyes, to gasp and sigh with her in her swooning anguish. . . . The light glimmers on her through blinding tears; she strives, as one has so often striven in a nightmare dream, to speak, but cannot; the actual kings are there, not phantoms or spectres, but stern men with black beards and wolfish eyes. Dimly, through burning tears, the whole scene quivers before her, 'the temples and the people and the shore,' and then, real as everything else is real, the knife is drawn slowly through her throat. The altered version is not merely inferior to the other, but, what by no means necessarily follows, is capable of being demonstrated to be inferior, by reference to simple and irrefragable principles of criticism. Is it permissible that Iphigenia should begin her narrative in such a fervor of imaginative passion that she no longer speaks of the scene or of herself, but *sees* the whole in vision; and should thus carry it on until it reaches its most agitating point; and should *then* sink back into the infinitely colder and less imaginative mood of one who speaks from memory, who coolly separates her present self from her past, and talks of herself as 'the victim'? She passes from poetic vision —'*I* strove to speak, *I* could descry,' — to prosaic recollection. If criticism has any principles at all, such a declension ruins the passage. The 'bright death' is due to the same unparalleled error. Seeing, as Tennyson originally saw, through the eyes of the swooning girl, the wolfish kings and flickering crowd, he had no leisure to think of 'bright death,' no idle ingenuity of spirit to hit upon such a conceit. 'Bright death'

* Warren and Corson speak of the change as having been made " in 1860; " but we suspect that it dates back to the ed. of 1853, as we find it in American reprints as early as 1856.

means nothing in particular, and would probably suggest a flash of lightning if the knife had not been mentioned in the earlier version. . . . If I live for a hundred years, I shall always *see*, with my mind's eye, those wolfish kings, those quivering masts, that shore, that crowd, and most clearly of all that knife, as they flashed on me when Tennyson showed me them in my boyhood; and it amazes me beyond measure that he should not resent, as I have resented, the attempt to dissolve the vision by intrusion of bright deaths and historical talk about victims."

On the other hand, Warren says: "The brilliant metonomy of 'bright death' vivifies the tamer 'sharp knife' with the electric touch of genius. The remainder of the verse is, we submit, rather weakened. The rapid and elliptical 'and nothing more' surely more vividly portrays the last flash of fainting consciousness than the slow-drawn action and deliberate phrasing of 'And I knew no more.'"

Rev. A. K. H. Boyd (*Fraser's Mag.* Feb. 1863) says that the original picture "passes the limits of tragedy, and approaches the physically revolting. It is, likewise, suggestive rather of the killing of a sheep or pig than of the solemn sacrifice of a human being." Of the revised stanza he says: "You will see that it has been most severely cut and carved; but to a most admirable result. . . . This is as though a piece of baser metal were touched with the philosopher's stone, and turned to gold."

For ourself, we fully agree with Bayne. Tennyson's alterations are almost invariably improvements, but this seems to us one of the most glaring exceptions to the rule. The change from the first to the third person is a fall from poetry to prose, and *bright death* is only a stepping-stone that eases the descent. There was, moreover, a pathetic self-pity in *my tender throat* which we are sorry to lose.

118. *Heavy-plunging.* Cf. *Palace of Art*, 251 above.

127. *A queen*, etc. Cleopatra. Corson quotes a writer in *Notes and Queries* (4th series, vol. x. p. 499): "How is Tennyson's description of Cleopatra, 'A queen, with swarthy cheeks, and bold black eyes,' to be reconciled with the fact that she was a Greek, the daughter of Ptolemy Auletes and a lady of Pontus, therefore of pure Greek blood?"

132. *Like the moon*, etc. Mr. J. C. Carr compares *The Witch of Edmonton*, ii. 2:

"You are the powerful moon of my blood's sea,
    To make it ebb and flow into my face,
    As your looks change."

139. *Cæsar.* Octavius, whom she could not captivate.

145. *We drank*, etc. "The exultation of the wild witch-like woman when she thinks of her Antony is grand" (Bayne).

Shepherd (*Tennysoniana*, p. 10) quotes the following from the early version of the poem:

"O what days and nights
    We had in Egypt, ever reaping new
    Harvest of ripe delights!

> " What dainty strifes, when fresh from war's alarms,
>   My Hercules, my gallant Antony,
> My mailed captain, leapt into my arms,
>   Contented there to die.
>
> " And in those arms he died; I heard my name
>   Sigh'd forth with life : then I shook off all fear;
> O what a little snake stole Cæsar's fame !
>   What else was left? look here."

146. *Canopus.* The brightest star in the constellation Argo (except when the variable Eta Argus is at its maximum), and next to Sirius the brightest in the heavens.

155. *The other.* That is, Octavius.

A worm. Cf. Shakespeare, *A. and C.* v. 2. 243 :

> " Hast thou the pretty worm of Nilus there,
> That kills and pains not? "

161. *I died a queen,* etc. As Mr. Carr remarks, this passage is " a splendid *transfusion* " of the last lines in Horace's ode (i. 36) :

> " Invidens
> *Privata* deduci superbo
> *Non humilis* mulier triumpho."

177. *Undazzled.* Recovered from the dazzling effect; a word not found in the dictionaries, and perhaps coined by the poet.

181–188. *The torrent brooks,* etc. " How solemn, how true to the religious enthusiasm of a Hebrew maiden, are not only these verses, but all that ' the daughter of the warrior Gileadite' sings and says!" (Bayne.) It is Jephtha's daughter who sings. See *Judges,* xi. 29 fol. The Biblical narrative will explain the allusions in the following stanzas.

213. *No fair Hebrew boy,* etc. Among the Hebrews, as among Oriental nations generally, offspring, and especially male offspring, was reckoned a blessing and an honor, and its absence a misfortune and disgrace. According to some eminent commentators, Jephtha's daughter was not put to death but devoted to a life of virginity.

225. *Saw God divide the night,* etc. Cf. Horace, *Od.* i. 34 :

> " Diespiter
> Igni corusco nubila dividens."

243. *Thridding.* This old form of *thread* is used also in *Princess,* iv. 242 : " To thrid the musky-circled mazes ; " and in *In Mem.* 97 : " He thrids the mazes of the mind."

For *boscage* (= sylvan growth) cf. *Sir John Oldcastle:* " Rather to thee, green boscage, work of God." In *Princess,* i. 110 we find " blowing bosks " (thickets) ; and Shakespeare and Milton use the adjective *bosky.* See *Princess,* p. 154.

251. *Rosamond,* etc. Stow says : " Rosamond the fayre daughter of Walter Lord Clifford, concubine to Henry II. (poisoned by Queen Elianor, as some thought) dyed at Woodstocke [A.D. 1177], where king Henry had made for her a house of wonderfull working; so that no man or woman might come to her, but he that was instructed by the

king, or such as were right secret with him touching the matter. . . .
It was commonly said, that lastly the queene came to her by a clue of
thridde, or silke, and so dealt with her, that she lived not long after:
but when she was dead she was buried at Godstow, in an house of
nunnes beside Oxford, with these verses upon her tombe:

> Hic jacet in tumba Rosa mundi, non Rosa munda :
> Non redolet, sed olet, quae redolere solet."

Cf. the ballad of *Fair Rosamond* in Percy's *Reliques.*

359. *Fulvia's waist.* Cleopatra puts the name of *Fulvia*, the wife of
her paramour Antony, for that of Eleanor, the wife of Rosamond's
royal paramour.

363. *The captain of my dreams.* Venus, the morning star. The goddess of love and beauty may well enough be called the *captain* — the
leader or inspirer — of the poet's dreams of fair women. Corson makes
it mean "the sun;" but, as we understand the context, the sun has not
yet risen. The first beams of the dawn have appeared, and are broad-
ening and brightening in the east. The morning star is up, but the
darkness is not yet dispersed by the sunrise. Besides, the sun could be
called the *captain* of his dreams only in the sense of controlling or
checking them; and this seems rather forced and far-fetched.

366. *Her, who clasp'd*, etc. Margaret Roper, the daughter of Sir
Thomas More. After his execution his head was exposed on London
Bridge, but she obtained permission to take it down, and, after preserv-
ing it as a precious relic till her death, was buried with it in her arms.

369. *Or her who knew*, etc. Eleanor, queen of Edward I. of England, who accompanied her husband to the Holy Land in 1269. There
he was stabbed in the arm with a dagger which was believed to have
been poisoned; and Eleanor instantly applied her lips to the wound
and sucked the blood until the surgeons were ready to dress it.

THE EPIC: MORTE D'ARTHUR.

THIS poem was first published in 1842, and was slightly retouched in
subsequent editions. The *Morte d'Arthur* has been incorporated, with
no other change than the omission of a single line (see on 58 below)
in *The Passing of Arthur,* the last of the *Idyls of the King;* but it has
continued to be included, with the original introduction and conclu-
sion, in the complete editions of Tennyson.

The poem would appear to have been written as early as 1837.
Landor writes under date of December 9, 1837, as follows: "Yesterday a Mr. Moreton, a young man of rare judgment, read to me a manu-
script by Mr. Tennyson, very different in style from his printed poems.
The subject is the death of Arthur. It is more Homeric than any
poem of our time, and rivals some of the noblest parts of the Odyssea "
(Forster's *Life of Landor,* ii. 323).

3. *The sacred bush.* The mistletoe.

27. *You know, said Frank,* etc. The first reading (retained till 1846) was:

> " ' You know,' said Frank, ' he flung
> His epic of King Arthur in the fire! ' "

37. *And why,* etc. The reading in the eds. of 1842 and 1843 was:

> " and why should any man
> Remodel models rather than the life?
> And these twelve books of mine (to speak the truth)
> Were faint Homeric echoes," etc.

52. *So all day long,* etc. Stedman says: "To my mind, there is a marked difference in style between the original and later portions of this work [the *Idyls*]. The *Morte d'Arthur* of 1842 is Homeric to the farthest degree possible in the slow, Saxon movement of the verse; grander, with its 'hollow oes and aes,' than any succeeding canto, always excepting *Guinevere.*"

58. *Sir Bedivere, the last,* etc. This line is omitted in the *Idyls.*

63. *A great water.* "This phrase has probably often been ridiculed as affected phraseology for 'a great lake;' but it is an instance of the intense presentative power of Mr. Tennyson's genius. It precisely marks the appearance of a large lake outspread and taken in at one glance from a high ground. Had 'a great lake' been substituted for it, the phrase would have needed to be translated by the mind into water of a certain shape and size, before the picture was realized by the imagination. 'A great *lake*' is, in fact, one degree removed from the sensuous to the logical, — from the individual appearance to the generic name, and is, therefore, less poetic and pictorial " (Brimley).

72. *Camelot.* See on *Lady of Shalott,* 5 above.

82. *Samite.* A rich silk stuff. Cf. Spenser, *F. Q.* iii. 12. 13: "In silken samite she was light arayd," etc.

89. *Seest.* Printed "seëst" in all the eds., indicating that the poet wants the dissyllabic pronunciation preserved. See the remarks on Tennyson's metre in *Princess,* p. 142 fol.

94. *Hest.* Not to be printed '*hest,* as if a contraction of *behest.* Shakespeare uses it oftener than *behest;* as in *Temp.* i. 2. 274, iii. 1. 37, iv. 1. 65, etc.

102. *The shining levels.* "The classical *aequora* may have suggested the 'shining *levels,*' but there is a deeper reason for the change of phrase, for the 'great water,' as seen from the high ground, becomes a series of flashing surfaces when Sir Bedivere looks along it from its margin " (Brimley).

107. *Diamond sparks.* The eds. down to 1853 have "diamond studs."

111. *This way and that,* etc. A translation of Virgil, *Æn.* iv. 285: "Atque animum nunc huc celerem, nunc dividit illuc."

115. *Marge.* Cf. *Recoll. of Arab. Nights,* 59 above.

121. *I heard the ripple,* etc. As Brimley remarks, "the 'ripple *washing in the reeds,*' and the 'wild water *lapping on the crags,*' are two phrases marking exactly the difference of sound produced by water swelling up against a permeable or impermeable barrier."

131. *Lief.* Loved, beloved. Cf. Spenser, *F. Q.* i. 3. 28: "Then I leave you, my liefe, yborn of heavenly berth;" *Id.* i. 9. 17: "worthie to be her liefe;" *Id.* iii. 2. 33: "tell me therefore, my liefest liefe," etc.

134. *Across the ridge,* etc. This line was inserted in 1853.

172. *Authority forgets a dying king,* etc. As Brimley says, this is "thoroughly Shakespearian." "The personification assists the imagination without distressing the understanding, as when dwelt upon, and expanded in detail; deepening the impressiveness of the sentiment by giving along with a true thought a grand picture, — just such a passing flash of impassioned rhetoric as would become the highest oratory, and thrill through the hearts of a great assembly."

181. *For.* Because; a common Elizabethan use of the word. Often it differs little from our looser conjunctional *for* (= because); but the difference is serious in a case like Shakespeare's *M. for M.* ii. 1. 27:

> "You may not so extenuate his offence,
> For I have had such faults;"

that is, the fact that I have been guilty is no excuse for him. Here the modern *for* would make nonsense of the passage.

183. *I will arise and slay thee.* As Forman remarks, this line is "one of the master touches of a masterly poem."

188. *Made lightnings,* etc. "A series of brilliant effects is hit off in those two words, *made lightnings. Whirl'd in an arch* is a splendid instance of sound answering to sense, which the older critics made so much use of; the additional syllable which breaks the measure, and necessitates an increased rapidity of utterance, seeming to express to the ear the rush of the sword up its parabolic curve. And with what lavish richness of presentative power is the boreal aurora, the collision, the crash, and the thunder of the meeting icebergs, brought before the eye! An inferior artist would have shouted through a page, and emptied a whole pallet of color, without any result but interrupting his narrative, where Tennyson in three lines strikingly illustrates the fact he has to tell, — associates it impressively with one of nature's grandest phenomena, and gives a complete picture of this phenomenon besides" (Brimley).

190. *The northern morn.* The *aurora borealis.* See on *Dream of Fair Women*, 27 above.

220. *Looking wistfully . . . as in a picture.* Mr. Carr compares Æschylus, *Agamemnon*, 230:

> ἔβαλλ' ἕκαστον
> ἀπ' ὄμματος βέλει φιλοίκτῳ
> πρέπουσα θ 'ὡς ἐν γραφαῖς.

242. *Lo! the level lake,* etc. See on *Dream of Fair Women*, 76 above. See also 267 below.

250. *Shiver'd to the tingling stars.* "In some over-fastidious moods, we might be inclined to charge this with a touch of that exaggeration which belongs to the 'spasmodic school;' but the cry comes from a company of spirits, amid mountains whose natural power of echo is heightened by the silence of night, the clearness of the wintry air, and the hardening effect of frost. Such a cry at such a time and in such a place would thrill from rock to rock, from summit to summit, till it seemed to pierce the sky in a hurtling storm of multitudinous arrowy sounds, and die away in infinitely distant pulsations among the stars " (Brimley).

253. *Where no one comes*, etc. " This passage may seem at first to add nothing to the force of the comparison, as the shrillness of the wind would not be greater in an uninhabited place than anywhere else in open ground. But the mournfulness of the feeling a man would experience in such a place, from the sense of utter isolation and sterility, is blended with the naturally sad wail of the wind over a wide waste, and the addition thus becomes no mere completion of a thought of which only part is wanted for the illustration — though that were allowable enough, according to ordinary poetic usage, — but gives a heightening of sentiment without which the illustration itself would be incomplete and less impressive " (Brimley).

266. *Cuisses.* Armor for the thighs; also spelt *cuishes.* Cf. Shakespeare, 1 *Hen. IV.* iv. 1. 105:

> " I saw young Harry with his beaver on,
> His cuisses on his thighs, gallantly arm'd," etc.

" The passage is a fine instance of a poetical use of simile and figure. The moon fading in the early morning, the dazzling brightness of the rising sun, the shattered column, the glancing flight of a shooting star, bring before the mind not only the dying king, pale and bleeding, but the contrast between his present weakness and the glory and triumphs of his chivalrous and brilliant life. In a few lines his whole story is told: it is not merely a dying warrior who lies before us, but the strength, the state, the splendor, and enjoyment of his past life flash before the imagination, and deepen the sadness and humiliation of his defeat and death " (Brimley).

305. *For so the whole round earth*, etc. Mr. Carr remarks that these two fine lines are the versification of a sentence from Archdeacon Hare's sermon on *The Law of Self-Sacrifice*: " This is the golden chain of love, whereby the whole creation is bound to the throne of the Creator."

310. *Avilion.* See on *Palace of Art*, 105 above.

353. *That.* So that; as often in Elizabethan English. Cf. Shakespeare, *J. C.* i. 1. 50:

> " Have you not made an universal shout,
> That Tiber trembled underneath her banks," etc.

THE TALKING OAK.

ONLY two slight changes (the author of *Tennysoniana* says "one") have been made in the poem since its first appearance in 1842.

Mr. J. Hutchison (*St. Paul's Magazine*, Oct. 1873) remarks : " Landor himself, in his happiest vein, never conceived a more exquisite imaginary conversation. Here in sportive phrase and bantering talk, is the whole philosophy of forest-life set forth with a poetic felicity, saucy humor, and scientific precision of language, each admirable of its kind. The poem is literally a love-idyl and botanic treatise combined, and never surely were lovers and science — January and May, might one say — so delightfully harmonized; conveying, too, to those who have eyes to see and hearts to understand, glimpses of a spiritual interpretation of nature, undreamt of by Pope and his school. . . . Seldom has the imagery of the woods been used with more appropriateness and effect than in this poem, and its poetic excellence is rivalled by its accuracy. No one but an accomplished practical botanist could have written it."

Stedman calls the poem "that marvel of grace and fancy, that nonpareil of sustained lyrics in quatrain verse; as exquisite in filigree-work as *The Rape of the Lock*, with an airy beauty and rippling flow, compared with which the motion of Pope's couplets is that of partners in an eighteenth-century minuet."

11. *That makes me thrice a man.* Cf. *The Miller's Daughter*, 93–96.

47. *Bluff Harry.* Henry VIII.; his daughter Elizabeth being the *man-minded offset* of 51 below.

54. *That wild wind.* The violent storm of the night when Cromwell died. Some of the biographers of the Protector have asserted that his father was a brewer; but this is very improbable, and does not justify the poet in calling the son a *brewer*, which he certainly never was.

57. *She-slips.* All the old oak's metaphors are drawn from his own arboreal life and associations. The poet thinks as a tree and speaks as a tree, putting off his human nature for the nonce.

63. *In teacup times*, etc. In the days of Queen Anne. The artificial and affected pastoral poetry of that time is well hit off in the next stanza.

69. *May insects prick.* The gall-flies. The oak *feels* the irritant fluid which the insect is supposed to prick into the leaf when it inserts its egg, and which causes the formation of the *gall*.

89. *For as to fairies.* The big burly old fellow can hardly sympathize with creatures so delicate as the fairies. His character is as admirably sustained throughout as any in Shakespeare.

107. *Oxlip.* The *Primula elatior*, or "greater cowslip." Cf. Shakespeare, *W. T.* iv. 4. 125: "bold oxlips; " and Drayton, *Polyolbion*, xv.:

> "To sort these flowers of showe, with other that were sweet,
> The cowslip then they couch, and th' oxlip for her meet."

123. *Holt.* Wood or woodland; seldom used except in poetry. Cf. *Locksley Hall*, 191 below.

132. *And turn'd to look at her.* A touch that adds a new charm to the old figure.

145. *Yet seem'd*, etc. How subtly the poet gives a half-human sensibility to the garrulous veteran of the forest without violence to his real nature! His "sense of touch" remains "somewhat coarse," he is still

" hard wood and wrinkled rind," and the pleasure he feels is at best only like the " blind motions " of his renewed life in the spring-time.

148. *The berried briony.* The *Bryonia dioica*, a common plant in England, bearing red berries about the size of a pea. Cf. *The Brook*, 203 below.

181. *I, rooted here*, etc. Only a botanist can appreciate the blended poetry and science of this stanza.

185. *For ah! my friend*, etc. The original reading was " For ah ! the Dryad-days were brief," etc.

199. *Pursue thy loves*, etc. This making the lover become a little jealous when the oak grows so warm as to talk of "kiss for kiss " is as true to nature as it is humorous.

215. *The murmurs.* The early reading is " The whispers."

264. *Lizard-point.* The southernmost point of Great Britain, some twenty-three miles to the southeast of the Land's End.

275. *The northern morning.* The *aurora borealis*. See on *Morte d'Arthur*, 190 above.

292. *That Thessalian growth.* The oak grove in Dodona (in Epirus, not in the neighboring Thessaly), where the black dove, flying from Thebes in Egypt, alighted, and proclaimed that there an oracle of Jupiter should be established.

297. *The younger Charles.* Charles I. The story is a familiar one.

ULYSSES.

FIRST published in 1842, and unaltered since.

Mr. Carr says : " The germ, the spirit, and the sentiment of this poem are from the 26th canto of Dante's *Inferno*. Mr. Tennyson has indeed done little but fill in the sketch of the great Florentine. As is usual with him in all cases where he borrows, the details and minuter portions of the work are his own ; he has added grace, elaboration, and symmetry ; he has called in the assistance of other poets. A rough crayon draught has been metamorphosed into a perfect picture. As the resemblances lie not so much in expression as in general tone, we will in this case substitute for the original a literal version. Ulysses is speaking :

" ' Neither fondness for my son, nor reverence for my aged sire, nor the due love which ought to have gladdened Penelope, could conquer in me the ardor which I had to become experienced in the world, and in human vice and worth. I put out into the deep open sea with but one ship, and with that small company which had not deserted me. . . . I and my companions were old and tardy. When we came to that narrow pass where Hercules assigned his landmarks, " O brothers," I said, " who through a hundred thousand dangers have reached the West, deny not to this the brief vigil of your senses that remain, experience of the unpeopled world beyond the sun. Consider your origin ; ye are not formed to live like brutes, but to follow virtue and knowledge." . . . Night already saw the other pole with all its stars, and ours so low that it rose not from the ocean floor.'"

R. H. Horne (*New Spirit of the Age*, 1843) says of the poem: "The mild dignity and placid resolve — the steady wisdom after the storms of life, and with the prospect of future storms — the melancholy fortitude, yet kingly resignation to his destiny which gives him a restless passion for wandering — the unaffected and unostentatious modesty and self-conscious power — the long softened shadows of memory cast from the remote vistas of practical knowledge and experience, with a suffusing tone of ideality breathing over the whole, and giving a saddened charm even to the suggestion of a watery grave — all this, and much more, independent of the beautiful picturesqueness of the scenery, render the poem of *Ulysses* one of the most exquisite in the language."

Bayne remarks: "Antithetically and grandly opposed to the nerveless sentiment of *The Lotos-Eaters* is the masculine spirit of the lines on Ulysses, one of the healthiest as well as most masterly of all Tennyson's poems."

In a like vein, Stedman declares that "for virile grandeur and astonishingly compact expression, there is no blank-verse poem, equally restricted as to length, that approaches the *Ulysses:* conception, imagery, and thought are royally imaginative, and the assured hand is Tennyson's throughout."

Margaret Fuller writes in August, 1842: "I have just been reading the new poems of Tennyson. . . . One of his themes has long been my favorite — the last expedition of Ulysses — and his, like mine, is the Ulysses of the Odyssey, with his deep romance of wisdom, and not the worldling of the Iliad. How finely marked his slight description of himself and of Telemachus!"

10. *The rainy Hyades.* The well-known group of stars in the head of Taurus. Cf. Virgil, *Æn.* i. 748: "Arcturum, pluviasque Hyadas, geminosque Triones."

16. *Delight of battle.* "What a superb translation of the *certaminis gaudia* of the Latin poet!" (Bayne.)

22. *How dull it is,* etc. Shepherd (*Tennysoniana*, p. 87) notes the "remarkable resemblance of thought and expression" to a speech of Ulysses in Shakespeare's *T. and C.* iii. 3. 150:

> " Perseverance, dear my lord,
> Keeps honor bright. To have done is to hang
> Quite out of fashion, like a rusty mail
> In monumental mockery," etc.

"The old sea-king, strong as a fishing-boat that has battled long with tide and storm, spurns the idea of rest" (Bayne).

39. *Most blameless is he,* etc. "Excellent young man! — but what an unspeakable relief it will be never to hear his judicious remarks again! A wilder set of fellows I have been accustomed to:

> My mariners,
> Souls that have toil'd and wrought and thought with me . . .

We need not quarrel with Tennyson for having bestowed those mariners on Ulysses in his old age. There were, indeed, none such. They all lay fathom-deep in brine ; no Homer, no Athene, had paid regard to *them ;* Ulysses returned alone to his isle, the hero only being of account in the eyes of classic poet or Pagan goddess. Tennyson's Ulysses is, after all, an Englishman of the Nelson wars rather than a Greek, and his feeling for his old salts is a distinctively Christian sentiment. So, indeed, is his desire for effort, discovery, labor, to the end. It never would have occurred to Homer that Ulysses could want anything for the rest of his life but pork-chops and Penelope " (Bayne).

LOCKSLEY HALL.

THE poem has been altered but little since its first appearance in 1842.

Bayne remarks : " It is, I fancy, to *Locksley Hall,* more than to any other of his poems, that Tennyson owes his hold upon the heart of the world. Partly this may be due to its being a peculiarly fascinating and piquant variation from his usual manner. It is *trochaic* in melody, the beat coming upon the first syllable in the metrical foot instead of, as in the iambus, on the second. The corresponding iambic measure, in which the beat falls on the second syllable, is exhibited in Macaulay's *Lays of Ancient Rome :*

> Then Ocnus of Falerii rush'd on the Roman three,
> And Lausalus of Urgo, the rover of the sea.

" Tennyson generally uses the iambus. This is, indeed, the organic unit of measurement in English verse, forming the basis of the heroic stanza, rhymed and unrhymed, as employed in all the monumental works of English poetry. . . . So long ago as the days of Aristotle the iambic measure was considered 'the natural march-music of action and business.' It is most consistent with the genius of the English tongue, and Tennyson has evidently found it harmonize best with that patient elaboration, that minute and symmetrical working up of the pictures of his mind, in which he delights. In *Locksley Hall,* however, he gives voice to one of those high tides of emotion in which the full heart sometimes relieves itself, and on such an occasion it was more important to render the force and billowy splendor of the waves, to express sympathy with their glorious freedom, their magnificent boldness, and wildness, and tumult, their clapping of hands and revelry of infinite laughter, or passionate sobbing of grief, than to mould their particular forms or to time their march upon the beach. In *Locksley Hall,* therefore, Tennyson escapes from that iambic regularity, that dignified perfection and repose, so characteristic of his general manner, into the fitful and ringing, or wildly wailing and throbbing, melody of a trochaic measure."

Brimley (*Cambridge Essays*, 1855) says: " It is against the fickleness of a woman . . . that the speaker in *Locksley Hall* has to find a resource. And he finds it in the excitement of enterprise and action, in glowing anticipations of progress for the human race. He not merely recovers his sympathy with his fellow-men, and his interest in life, which had been paralyzed by the unworthiness of her who represented for him all that was beautiful and good in life, — but he recovers it on higher and firmer ground. What he lost was a world that reflected his own unclouded enjoyment, his buoyant ardor and high spirits; a world appreciated mainly in its capacity for affording variety to his perceptive activity and scope for his unflagging energies; a world of which he himself, with his pleasures and his ambitions, was the centre. What he gains is a world that is fulfilling a divine purpose, beside which his personal enjoyments are infinitely unimportant, but in aiding and apprehending which his true blessedness is purified and deepened; a world in which he is infinitely small and insignificant, but greater in his brotherhood with the race which is evolving ' the idea of humanity ' than in any possible grandeur of his own. The poem has been called 'morbid,' a phrase that has acquired a perfectly new meaning of late years, and is made to include works of art, and all views of life that are colored by other than comfortable feelings. If *Locksley Hall*, as a whole, is morbid, then it is morbid to represent a young man rising above an early disappointment in love, and coming out from it stronger, less sensitive, more sinewed for action.

" What has led certain critics to call the poem morbid is, of course, that the speaker's judgment of his age, in the earlier part, is colored by his private wrong and grief. But it is not morbid, on the contrary, it is perfectly natural and right that outrages on the affections should disturb the calmness of the judgment, that acts of treacherous weakness should excite indignation and scorn; and the view of the world natural to this state of mind is quite as true as that current upon the Stock Exchange, and not at all more partial or prejudiced. It is not, indeed, the highest, any more than it is a complete view, but it is higher and truer than the ' all serene ' contemplation of a comfortable Epicurean or passionless thinker. There is no cynicism in the 'fine curses' of *Locksley Hall ;* they are not the poisonous exhalations of a corrupted nature, but the thunder and lightning that clear the air of what is foul, the forces by which a loving and poetical mind, not yet calmed and strengthened by experience and general principles, repels unaccustomed outrage and wrong. With what a rich emotion he recalls his early recollections! Sea, sandy shore, and sky have been for him a perpetual fountain of beauty and of joy, his youth a perpetual feast of imaginative knowledge and pictorial glory. With what a touching air of tenderness and protection he watches the young girl whom he loves in secret, and whose paleness and thinness excite his pity as well as his hope! How rapturously, when she avows her love, he soars up in his joy with a flight that would be tumultuous but for the swiftness of the motion, — unsteady but for the substantial massiveness of thought, and the grand poising sweep of the lyric power that sustains it! Then how pathetic the sudden fall, the modulation by which he passes from the key of rapture to that of despair! And here and there, through all that storm of anger, sarcasm, contempt, denunciation, that follows, there sounds a note of unutterable tenderness which gives to the whole movement a prevailing character of pain and anguish, of moral desolation, rather than of wrath and vengeance. Not till this mood exhausts itself, and the mind of the speaker turns to action as a resource against despair, does he realize all that he has lost. Not only is his love uprooted, — his hope, his faith in the world, have perished in that lightning flash ; and he turns again to his glorious youth, but now only to sound the gulf that separates him from it. The noble aspirations, the ardent hopes, the sanguine prophecies of earlier years roll in rich pomp of music and of picture before us ; but it is the cloud-pageantry of the boy's day-dream which breaks up to reveal the world as it appears now to the 'palsied heart' and 'jaundiced eye' of the man. Yet in the midst of this distempered vision are seen glimpses of a deeper truth. The eternal law of progress is not broken because the individual man is shipwrecked. It is but a momentary glimpse, and offers no firm footing. His personal happiness, after all, is what concerns each person. Here, at least, in this convention-ridden, Mammon-worshipping Europe, where the passions are cramped, and action that would give scope to passionate energy impossible, the individual has no chance. But in some less advanced civilization, where the individual is freer if the race be less forward, there may be hope. And a picture of the tropics rises before the imagination, dashed off in a few strokes of marvellous breadth and richness of color. But the deeper nature of the man controls the delusion of the fancy; his heart, reason, and conscience revolt against the escape into a mere savage freedom; they will not allow him to drop out of the van of the advancing host; and manly courage comes with the great thought of a society that is rapidly fulfilling the idea of humanity; the personal unhappiness, the private wrong, the bitterness of outraged affection, give way before the upswelling sympathy with the triumph of the race to which he belongs. The passion has passed in the rush of words that gave it expression, and life shines clear again, no longer on the tender-hearted, imaginative boy, but on the man

> Made weak by time and fate, but strong in will,
> To strive, to seek, to find, and not to yield. "

3. *'T is the place, and all around it*, etc. The reading of 1842 is: " 'T is the place, and round the gables," etc.

4. *Dreary gleams.* The construction of *gleams* has been much discussed. We have always regarded it as in apposition with *curlews.* The birds as they fly over the hall, seem like *dreary gleams* in the sky. Some have assumed that *curlew's call* is the subject of *gleams ;* and they compare Sophocles: ἔλαμσε ἀρτίως φανεῖσα φάμα ; and Pindar: βοὰ πρέπει.

5. *Locksley Hall, that in the distance overlooks*, etc. This is the original

reading, changed in the *Selections* of 1865 to " Locksley Hall, that half in ruin overlooks," etc., but afterwards restored.

8. *Sloping.* See on *Palace of Art*, 247 above.

14. *Closed.* Enclosed, included. Cf. *Princess*, concl. 94:

> " few words and pithy, such as closed
> Welcome, farewell," etc.

See note in our ed. p. 187.

31. *Love took up the glass of Time*, etc. Mr. Carr compares, but mis-quotes W. R. Spencer:

> " How noiseless falls the foot of Time
> That only treads on flowers!
>
> And who with clear account remarks
> The ebbing of his glass,
> When all its sands are diamond sparks
> That dazzle as they pass?"

34. *Smote the chord of self*, etc. " This line concentrates into itself a large part of Tennyson's noble conception of love, or conception of the nobleness of love. Love annihilates Self, even while exalting it, and crowns life in a two-fold ecstasy of renunciation and attainment. A life of unselfish, beneficent occupation — of sympathy in mental culture — of co-operation in benevolent effort — would have been the natural sequel. But Mammon and conventional respectability tore the strings from the harp of Life, and shattered the glass of Time with its golden sands " (Bayne).

38. *And our spirits*, etc. Mr. Carr remarks that this looks like a reminiscence of Guarini's *Pastor Fido*, ii. 6:

> " Ma i colpi di due labbra innamorate,
> Quando a ferir si va bocca con bocca,
> . . . ove l'un alma e l'altra
> Corre."

47. *As the husband is*, etc. The same critic says that this recalls Scott's *Abbot*, chap. ii.: " Know that the rank of the man rates that of the wife."

63. *Well — 'tis well that I should bluster!* " Exception has been taken to the tone which the discarded lover assumes toward her who has forsaken him, as if its harshness were impossible for a generous and magnanimous nature, which Tennyson, without question, intends his lover to be. But I think this is to bring the air of Rosa Matilda romance over the world of reality. It would have been very pretty for the poet to represent his lover as breathing nothing but admiration and broken-hearted forgiveness. Schiller might perhaps have told the story so; but Goethe or Shakespeare would not. Heroes that are too angelic cease to be men. The high-flown magnanimity is the sign-manual of the false sublime. Tennyson makes it plain also that it is only what is degrading in Amy's life that the lover blames and hates. Beneath all his angry words, his love for her remains ineradicable, and he would wish her happy if he could do so and at the same time save her from his contempt " (Bayne).

68. *Rookery.* Flock of rooks, or the birds that belong to a rookery. Cf. *Princess*, concl. 97 : " The long line of the approaching rookery."

72. *Whom to look at was to love.* Cf. Burns :

> " But to see her was to love her,
> Love but her, and love forever."

76. *That a sorrow's crown*, etc. This is from Dante, *Inf.* v. 121 :

> " Nessun maggior dolore
> Che ricordarsi del tempo felice
> Nella miseria."

121. *Argosies.* A name applied to the larger merchant ships of the olden time. Cf. Shakespeare, *M. of V.* i. 1. 9 : " your argosies with portly sail," etc.

129. *Of most.* That is, of the majority.

130. *Lapt.* Enfolded. Cf. *Princess*, ii. 151 :

> "lapt
> In the arms of leisure."

See our ed. p. 154.

135. *Slowly comes*, etc. " What a picture is this of Feudalism settling to its last sleep, with Freedom advancing upon it ! Or of aristocracies that nod and wink in the waning light of their heraldic honors, with the grand roar of the democracy beginning to be heard ! " (Bayne.)

138. *The process of the suns.* The lapse of years. Cf. Shakespeare, *Sonn.* 104. 6 : " In process of the seasons," etc.

162. *Swings.* The early reading was, " droops."

168. *I will take some savage woman*, etc. Mr. Carr remarks that " the cynical aspiration finds a curious parallel " in Beaumont's *Philaster*, iv. 2 :

> " O that I had been nourish'd in the woods,
> . . . and not known
> The right of crowns, nor the dissembling trains
> Of women's looks. . . .
> And then had taken me some mountain girl
> Beaten with winds, that might have strew'd my bed
> With leaves and reeds, and have borne at her big breasts
> My large coarse issue. This had been a life
> Free from vexation."

180. *Like Joshua's moon.* See *Joshua*, x. 12.

181. *Beacons.* The verb is rare.

182. *The great world.* The original reading is " the peoples."

183. *The globe.* The early reading is " the world."

184. *Cycle.* Used of course for an indefinitely long period, or an age. Cf. *Two Voices*, 17. Some criticaster has urged the objection that a Chinese " cycle " is less than fifty years (we forget the precise length) ; and somebody else takes the *cycle* to be the Platonic " great year."

Cathay was the name given to China by the old travellers. *Cataia* was another form of it, whence *Cataian*, used as a term of contempt by Shakespeare (*M. W.* ii. 1. 148, *T. N.* ii. 3. 80), Davenant, and other old writers.

191. *Holt.* See on *Talking Oak*, 123.

THE TWO VOICES.

FIRST published in the edition of 1842 (where it is dated 1833), and unaltered except in line 457.

Bayne remarks : " It is required of all poetry, without exception, that it be lovely and picture-like to the eye, and tuneful to the ear.   These conditions cannot be relaxed in favor of metaphysical poetry.   Since, therefore, metaphysical truth is truth in its most abstract form, it will clearly result that to produce in one and the same work good metaphysics and delightful poetry is a matter of extreme difficulty.   This difficulty Tennyson has signally vanquished in *The Two Voices.*   It is a compact, closely-reasoned metaphysical essay on the worth of life and the hope of immortality, and yet I know no poem of Tennyson's more variegated in color, more piquantly and brilliantly picturesque, more truly though gravely melodious."

Tainsh says : " *The Two Voices* is a philosophical poem of the strictest kind.   It is one sustained argument, or a series of arguments upon the same subject, from the beginning to almost the close.   Yet it is full of luscious poetry.   It would be difficult to find another poem in which a conception so purely intellectual is clothed with such richness of imagination and imagery.   The argument is concerning suicide.   To feel the full force of it, it is necessary to separate one's self, for the time, from all that Christianity has taught us concerning the duty of patient endurance and the absolute surrender of the human will to the divine, concerning the lovingness of God, and the ' soul of good in things evil,' and to take up the position of, say, a high-souled Greek whose life was full enough of sadness and suffering to have become a burden to him.   From such a situation the argument starts.   The sinfulness of suicide is out of the question — that is not showable except on Christian grounds.   The question of the poem is whether on natural grounds suicide could be defended, or must be condemned."

We add the analysis of the poem by the same author :

" *Voice.*   You are so miserable, why not die ?
Man.   This being of mine is too wonderful to be wantonly destroyed.
Voice.   A dragon-fly is more wonderful than you.
Man.   Not so.   The pre-eminence of man lies in his intellectual and moral nature.
Voice.   You are proud.   Let me grant that you are higher than the fly and some other beings.   Think you there are not many other beings in the universe higher than you ?
(*resumes.*) Moreover, you are but one of many.   There would be plenty of men like you left.
Man.   No two beings are altogether alike.
Voice.   Even so, among millions of shades of difference, will your particular shade be missed ?
Man.   You cannot know.

" This is the end of the first argument.   It might seem weak on the side of the man, but it is not so.   The strength of the temptation depends upon the truth of those things insinuated by the Voice.   The proof of the truth is challenged, and is not produced.   It is enough. Even a doubt upon this point would forbid suicide to a noble mind.   A new argument commences : —

Voice. You are so miserable and so impotent, 't were better to die.

Man. Matters may mend. If I die, I lose that chance.

Voice. What are the means of cure?

Man (not answering directly). If I should die, I should leave beautiful nature, and the knowledge of human progress. These would continue, while I was absent and ignorant.

Voice. But this must happen some day, in any case.

Man. Human progress is unceasing. If I bide my time, I see some of it.

Voice. The progress of man is so slow, so slight, compared with the infinite distance of the goal, that thousands of years would not suffice to show you any appreciable advance. How much less will some thirty years avail! Moreover, *you* cannot watch and see even this fancied progress for want of health of body and calm of mind.

Man (again changing the argument). Men will call me a coward if I die rather than wait and suffer.

Voice. Much more a coward are you, then, to live; for so you are twice a coward: you fear the pain of life, yet dare not escape, because you fear the scorn of men. Moreover, does love so bind you to men that you need care for their scorn? Will it disturb your rest? In truth, they will not scorn you; they will forget you.

Man. That men will forget me is small inducement to put myself out of their sight. Rather it provokes me to live and recall the hope I once had of compelling them to remember me by useful and noble deeds done on their behalf.

Voice. Such dreams are common to youth. They pass as age advances. They are not worth preserving. Man cannot really do anything worth doing, or know anything worth knowing. The end of life is disappointment. Death is the remedy.

Man. That men *can* do and know is certain; for men have done and known.

Voice. Perhaps; or they thought so. Some men have happy temperaments: from such come happy phantasies.

Man (changing the argument once more). This life is bad. Should I seek death as I am, the next, so entered, may be worse — its suffering deeper and more fixed.

Voice. Ponder the dead man, and tell me do you find evidence of any new life to fear?

Man. You cannot prove the dead are dead. It is true that the outward signs imply it. Why then do we not hold these signs conclusive? The fact that thus, against all outer reasons, we doubt, is evidence for the new life. The heart of man forebodes a mystery. He has conceived an eternity. He conceives, too, the ideal, which here he nowhere finds. He sees, dimly, a Divine Father and a Purpose working through the universe. He feels in himself a higher nature struggling with his lower being. These doubts and questionings must have answers somewhere. You cannot answer them. Counter doubts will not do it, for the first doubts would still remain. Thus by doubts you have assailed me, and by doubts you are foiled.

Voice (after a pause in the argument). You had a beginning; you sprung from nothing. Why should you not have an end, and pass to nothing?

Man. You do not show that to begin necessarily implies to end. But suppose I grant it, I do not know that at birth I began to be. Each being may have many phases of life. I do not remember my last stage of being — the change of state may involve forgetfulness. Moreover,

> As here we find in trances, men
> Forget the thing that happens, then
> Until they fall in trance again;

so, should my next state of being be like my last, I may then remember that last, though forgetting it in this. Or I may have fallen from a higher state of being, and the yearnings after the noble and the beautiful which flit through my mind may be traces of that higher life. Or I may have risen through and from lower forms, and then I might well have forgotten, for even here we forget the days of early immaturity. Or I may have existed as an unbodied essence, and then I must needs be incapable of memory;

> For Memory, dealing but with Time,
> And he with matter, should she climb
> Beyond her own material prime?

Moreover, there do haunt me what seem like reminiscences of a past life, as if what now seems new were not really new, but had been seen or done before.

Voice.

> The still voice laugh'd. ' I talk,' said he,
> ' Not with thy dreams! Suffice it thee
> Thy pain is a reality.'

Man. Yes, but you have missed your mark, and have not tricked me into death by one-sided falsehoods. No living being ever truly longed for death. It is more life that we want, not death.

" The battle is over, and the man has won the victory upon the ground chosen by the tempting voice. By the pleas common to all worthy humanity, suicide is irrational, weak, contemptible. The man is victorious, but not the less is he desolate;

> I ceased and sat as one forlorn.

But then comes the second voice whispering Christian hopes; and the sight of human love and worship, and the happy glory of nature, bring light and comfort to the desolate heart that, without light and comfort, had battled for the right."

7. *To-day I saw the dragon-fly*, etc. We are inclined to agree with Tainsh (see p. 186 above) in his interpretation of this reply of the Voice; and Mr. J. F. Genung (whose analysis of *In Memoriam* is the best we have) writes us that he has always explained the passage in the same way. Bayne understands the Voice to mean " that the shuffling off of this mortal coil may open to him new spheres of energy and happiness;" and that " the reply of the poet is that man is nature's highest product — the obvious suggestion being that there is no splendid dragon-fly into which the human grub, released by death, is likely to develop." But this "suggestion," so far from being "obvious," seems to us merely a desperate attempt to make the reference to the higher nature of man a "reply" to what the critic assumes that the Voice means to say. Corson, however, adopts this explanation.

33. *The kind.* That is, human kind; as the reply assumes.

34. *Response.* Accented on the first syllable. Cf. the throwing back of the accent in certain words by Shakespeare; as *relapse* in *Hen. V.* iv. 3. 107 : " Killing in relapse of mortality," etc.

39. *For thy deficiency.* At the loss of thee, or thy *peculiar difference.*

51. *But thou wilt weep.* That is, without weeping. The Voice "tries a new tack, and argues that the poet's wretchedness makes him unfit for anything but complaining " (Bayne).

53. *If I make dark.* Cf. *Job*, xiv. 20.

59. *The thorn.* The hawthorn. See on *The Miller's Daughter*, 130 above.

71. *The furzy prickle.* The prickly furze, or gorse.

74. *Is various to present.* Differs from its predecessors in presenting. This " indefinite use of the infinitive " (Abbott, *Shakes. Gr.* § 356) is common in Elizabethan English.

77. *Ruin'd tower.* "His own shattered selfhood from which he would take his outlook upon the world " (Corson).

85. *From his cold crown*, etc. From the snow-clad *summit overhead.*

103. *This is more vile*, etc. "The Voice sees its advantage, and attacks him sharply " (Bayne).

120. *Pride.* In the same construction as *resolve.*

125. *Among the tents,* etc. No doubt Corson is right in seeing here an allusion to the poet's university life.

170. *The riddle of the earth.* Cf. *Palace of Art,* 213 above.

173. *I told thee.* See 88–93 above. The Voice "recurs to the previously urged plea that man cannot read the riddle of the earth or grasp any truth related to the mind " (Bayne).

187. *Sometimes a little corner,* etc. The stanza bears a marked resemblance to a passage in *The Vale of Bones,* a piece in the *Poems by Two Brothers,* published in 1827 :

> "At times her partial splendor shines
> Upon the grove of deep black pines."

Another passage in the same poem is like one in *Oriana* (published in 1830), so that we can have no doubt which of the "Two Brothers" wrote it.

195. *Ixion-like.* Like Ixion, embracing a cloud when he thought to clasp a goddess in his arms.

198. *A little lower,* etc. See *Ps.* viii. 5.

204. *To flatter me,* etc. To delude me into suicide.

205. *I know that age to age,* etc. "He refers to the noble lives that have been lived, and maintains that, though the atmosphere of the world is darkened with dust of systems and of creeds, some have achieved calm, and known 'the joy that mixes man with heaven.' Here occurs that picture of the martyr Stephen which is in Tennyson's loftiest manner " (Bayne).

219. *Like Stephen.* In a poem *On the Death of my Grandmother* in the volume mentioned in the note on 187 above, these lines occur :

> " Her faith, like Stephen's, soften'd her distress ;
> Scarce less her anguish, scarce her patience less."

228. *The elements,* etc. Cf. Shakespeare, *J. C.* v. 5. 73 :

> " His life was gentle, and the elements
> So mix'd in him that Nature might stand up
> And say to all the world, ' This was a man !' "

and Drayton, *Baron's Wars,* ed. 1619 :

> " He was a man (then boldly dare to say)
> In whose rich soul the virtues well did suit,
> In whom so mixt the elements did lay
> That none to one could sovereignty impute ;
> As all did govern, so did all obey :
> He of a temper was so absolute,
> As that it seem'd, when Nature him began,
> She meant to show all that might be in man."

See our ed. of *J. C.* p. 185.

229. *I said, I toil beneath the curse,* etc. "The poet now suggests that, if he goes hence in quest of truth, he may merely exchange one riddle for a hundred, and that his anguish, 'unmanacled from bonds of sense,' may become permanent. On this, the Voice, reversing its original argument in favor of suicide, namely, that it might be the door to a

life of more splendid activity, tempts him with the prospect of eternal rest in death. Such inconsistency in argument is admirably in keeping with the character of a tempter " (Bayne).

Tainsh makes this "inconsistency in argument" a point against the explanation of 8–15 above which Bayne gives; but we think that the latter is right in regarding it as natural enough in a sophistical reasoner like the Voice.

256. *His sons grow up*, etc.   Mr. Carr compares *Job*, xiv. 20, 21.

264. *The place he knew*, etc.   Cf. *Job*, vii. 10.

277. *The simple senses*, etc.   To the senses the victory of Death seems complete and final.

280. *By these.* That is, by the senses.

283. *Forged.* Shaped, formed; as in Shakespeare, *A. IV.* i. 1. 85: " The best wishes that can be forged in your thoughts," etc.

Bayne remarks: " Here the poet has opened fire from his main battery. This is one of the grand arguments on which the advocate of immortality takes his stand. It is an argument pre-eminently accordant with modern science and modern philosophy, for no one can urge it with clearer logic than the evolutionist. Why is it proper for the bird to fly, and for the reptile to crawl? Because, says the evolutionist, the bird has developed wings. In like manner, the human creature has developed a faith in immortality, or, to put it at the lowest, a hope of immortality. Here and there a few persons, by elaborately educating themselves in the gospel of death, have quenched their hope of life beyond the grave; but that, throughout all the millions of civilized and semi-civilized humanity, this hope has been evolved, is just as sure as that a bird has wings. And .it adds greatly to the impressiveness of this hope that it has been evolved, as Tennyson specially urges, in clear antagonism to the main current of evidence that sense can produce upon the subject."

286. *He owns the fatal gift*, etc.   " He has the gift of inward spiritual eyes, which gift is 'fatal' to the verdict of the simple senses in regard to Death " (Corson).

287. *That read*, etc.   That recognize his spirit as having "intimations of immortality " — seeing, though only as in a glass darkly, its heritage of life beyond the grave.

292. *That type of Perfect*, etc.   " This is simply true, and it would be hard to name a truth of more importance. In the entire universe, as revealed to man by his senses, there is nothing perfect; and the central impulse in all man's noblest striving is derived from the aspiration of his spirit toward a perfect truth, a perfect beauty, a perfect happiness, which are exemplified nowhere in the world " (Bayne).

308. *His dark wisdom.*   Cf. the *blindly wise* in 287 above.

342. *That I first was*, etc.   That the beginning of my existence was, etc.

350. *Some draught of Lethe*, etc.   Cf. Virgil, *Æn.* vi. 748:

> " Has omnes, ubi mille rotam volvere per annos
> Lethaeum ad fluvium deus evocat agmine magno ;
> Scilicet immemores supera ut convexa revisant
> Rursus, et incipiant in corpora velle reverti."

See also Milton, *P. L.* ii. 582 :

> " Far off from these a slow and silent stream,
> Lethe, the river of oblivion, rolls
> Her watery labyrinth ; whereof who drinks
> Forthwith his former state and being forgets,
> Forgets both joy and grief, pleasure and pain."

371. *Unconfined.* Released, set free.

374. *Naked essence.* Spirit without a body.

379. *Moreover, something is or seems,* etc. As Mr. Carr remarks, these lines find an appropriate commentary in Wordsworth's *Ode on the Intimations of Immortality.*

389. *My mortal ark.* Corson quotes *In Mem.* 12 :

> " I leave this mortal ark behind,
> A weight of nerves without a mind."

401. *In quiet scorn.* Having no faith in the Sabbath as a symbol of heavenly rest.

406. *Soften'd airs.* The first mild winds of spring.

407. *Uncongeal.* "Note how much more significant this negative form is, in this place, than the positive form *thaw* would be " (Corson).

410. *Passing the place,* etc. The graveyard, which in England — at least, in rural England — is always the *churchyard,* surrounding the house of God.

445. *To feel,* etc. "The essence of the poem comes out here. All has been drifting to this central idea, namely, that the power to *feel* (not the power to *think*) is the safeguard of faith and hope and spiritual health " (Corson).

453. *You scarce could see,* etc. An English critic quotes George Peele, *Araynment of Paris :*

> " And rounde about the valley as ye passe,
> Ye may ne see, for peeping floures, the grasse."

457. *And all,* etc. The reading down to 1884 was " So variously seem'd all things wrought "

461. *Commune.* Accented on the first syllable ; as in Shakespeare, *Hamlet,* iv. 5. 202 : " Laertes, I must commune with your grief," etc.

ST. AGNES' EVE.

THIS poem first appeared in *The Keepsake* for 1837, and was slightly altered when reprinted in 1842. The title was changed from " St. Agnes " to " St. Agnes' Eve " in the edition of 1855.

16. *Argent round.* The moon. Cf. *Dream of Fair Women,* 158 above.

21. *Break up.* Break open ; as in 2 *Kings* xxv. 4, *Matt.* xxiv. 43, etc. Cf. also Shakespeare, 1 *Hen VI.* i. 3. 13 : " Break up the gates," etc.

SIR GALAHAD.

FIRST printed in 1842, and unaltered.

"*Sir Galahad* is a noble picture of a religious knight. He is almost as much a mystic as a soldier; both a monk and a warrior of the ideal type. He foregoes the world as much as if he lived within the monastery walls, and esteems his sword as sacred to the service of God as if it were a cross. His rapture is altogether that of the mystic. He is almost a St. Agnes, exchanging only the rapture of passivity for the transport of exultant effort. . . . He is just the embodiment of the noblest and the strongest tendencies of the chivalric age" (Tainsh).

5. *Shattering.* A peculiar but expressive use of the word. For *shrill-eth*, cf. *Princess*, v. 241 : "merrily-blowing shrill'd the martial fife," etc. See also *Talking Oak*, 68 above.

14. *On whom.* That is, on those on whom; an ellipsis common in Elizabethan English. Cf. Shakespeare, *M. for M.* ii. 2. 119: "Most ignorant of what he's most assur'd;" *R. of L.* 497: "And dotes on what he looks, 'gainst law or duty," etc.

42. *The Holy Grail.* This was the holy vessel from which our Saviour ate the paschal lamb at the Last Supper, or, as some said, out of which he dispensed the wine. It was said to have been brought to Britain by Joseph of Arimathea. See Spenser, *F. Q.* ii. 10. 53 :

> " Hither came Joseph of Arimathy,
> Who brought with him the holy grayle, they say."

When approached by any one not perfectly pure, it vanished from sight. Having been lost, it became the object of quest for knights-errant of all nations, and the legends of Arthur and the Knights of the Round Table were founded upon this legend of the search for it. Sir Galahad was at last successful in finding it.

THE BROOK.

THIS charming idyl was first published with *Maud* in 1855.

The brook of the poem is probably the one near Tennyson's birthplace in Somersby, Lincolnshire — the same which he describes in the *Ode to Memory*, one of his earliest poems, published in 1830 :

> "Come from the woods that belt the gray hillside,
> The seven elms, the poplars four,
> That stand beside my father's door,
> And chiefly from the brook that loves
> To purl o'er matted cress and ribbed sand,
> Or dimple in the dark of rushy coves,
> Drawing into his narrow earthen urn,
> In every elbow and turn
> The filter'd tribute of the rough woodland,
> O, hither lead thy feet ! "

4. *Scrip.* Certificates of stock.

6. *How money breeds.* Cf. Shakespeare, *M. of V.* i. 3. 95 :

> "*Antonio.* Was this inserted to make interest good?
> Or is your gold and silver ewes and rams?
> *Shylock.* I cannot tell; I make it breed as fast."

See also Bacon, *Essay on Usury:* "That it is against nature for money to beget money."

16. *Branding.* Burning, torrid.

17. *Neilgherry air.* The cool and salubrious Neilgherry Hills in India are the favorite summer resort of the British residents.

21. *O babbling brook*, etc. It has been suggested that the idea of this song of the brook was taken from a German lyric, *Das Bächlein:*

> "Du Bächlein, silberhell und klar,
>   Du eilst vorüber immerdar,
>
> Wo kommst du her? Wo gehst du hin?
> 'Ich komm' aus dunkler Felsen Schoss,
>   Mein Lauf geht über Blum' und Moss.' "

54. *Grigs.* Crickets; aptly described as *high-elbow'd.* According to Nares, the proverb, " as merry as a grig," is a corruption of " as merry as a *Greek*," which was an echo of the Roman proverbial reference to the fondness of the Greeks for good living and free potations.

70. *Lissome.* Lithe, lithesome; as in *Merlin and Vivien:* " her lissome limbs," etc.

80. *Makes a hoary eyebrow.* That is, by its arch.

118. *Meadow-sweet.* A common English plant, also called *meadow-wort,* the *Spiræa ulmaria* of the botanists.

130. *Shuddering.* Most aptly descriptive; as *twinkled* is in 135 just below.

138. *A long, long-winded tale.* The abstract of it which follows is full of humor.

176. *The netted sunbeam.* Another epithet that shows the poet's keen observation of little things in nature which few have eyes to see.

189. *The dome,* etc. The Duomo, or Cathedral of Florence, whose dome is the masterpiece of Brunelleschi.

194. *By the long wash,* etc. The poet is said to have specially prided himself on the sustained rhythmical quality of this line, as well he might. Bayard Taylor, however, thought it surpassed by Bryant's in *The Sea:*

> "The long wave rolling from the Southern Pole
> To break upon Japan."

203. *Briony.* See on *The Talking Oak,* 148.

ODE ON THE DEATH OF THE DUKE OF WELLINGTON.

THIS poem, originally published on the day of the Duke's funeral in 1852, was probably written in some haste. It underwent considerable revision before it was reprinted in 1853, and was further retouched before it appeared with *Maud* in 1855. We give *all* the variations of the present text from the 1st ed.

Shepherd, in his chapter on " Tennyson's versification," remarks : " In the *Ode on the Death of the Duke of Wellington*, he has soared to lyric heights to which, perhaps, even Pindar never attained. The tolling of the bell, the solemn and slow funeral march, the quick rush of battle, and the choral chant of the cathedral all succeed one another, and the verse sinks and swells, rises and falls to every alternation with equal power."

1. *Bury.* The 1st ed. has " Let us bury ; " as in 3 below.

5. *Mourning*, etc. The 1st ed. reads :

> " When laurel-garlanded leaders fall,
> And warriors carry," etc.

8. *Where shall we lay*, etc. After this line the ed. of 1853 has the following line, since suppressed : " He died on Walmer's lonely shore." The next line begins " But here," etc.

The reading of the 1st ed. was this :

> "Where shall we lay the man whom we deplore ?
> Let the sound of those he wrought for," etc.

20. *Remembering*, etc. The 1st ed. reads : " Our sorrow draws but on the golden Past ; " and it does not contain the next two lines.

28. *Clearest of.* The 1st ed. has " freest from."

42. *World-victor's victor.* The conqueror of Napoleon.

49. *The cross of gold.* On St. Paul's Cathedral, in the crypt of which the Duke is buried.

59. *Knoll'd.* This line is not in the 1st ed. Cf. *Macbeth*, v 8. 50 : " And so his knell is knoll'd."

74. *A man of well-attemper'd frame.* Cf. the quotation from *J. C.* in note on *Two Voices*, 228 above.

79. *Ever-echoing.* The reading down to 1873 was " ever-ringing."

80–82. *Who is he*, etc. The question is asked by the *mighty seaman*, Nelson, who is also buried in St. Paul's.

91. *His foes were thine*, etc. The 1st ed. reads : " His martial wisdom kept us free ; " and the following lines are :

> " O warrior-seaman, this is he,
> This is England's greatest son,
> Worthy of our gorgeous rites,
> And worthy to be laid by thee ;
> He that gain'd a hundred fights,
> And never lost an English gun ;
> He that in his earlier day
> Against the myriads of Assaye

> Clash'd with his fiery few and won :
> And underneath another sun
> Made the soldier, led him on,
> And ever great and greater grew,
> Beating from the wasted vines
> All their marshals' bandit swarms
> Back to France with countless blows ;
> Till their host of eagles flew
> Past the Pyrenean pines,
> Follow'd up," etc.

99. *Assaye.* A small town in Hindostan, memorable as the place where Wellington (then General Wellesley) began his career of victory, Sept. 23, 1803, by defeating an army of thirty thousand with a force of less than five thousand.

101. *Underneath another sun.* In Spain. The allusions to the famous campaign there need no comment.

118. *Such a war,* etc. After this line the 1st ed. has " He withdrew to brief repose ; " and then goes on with 119 as in the text.

123 *That loud Sabbath.* The day of Waterloo.

151. *A people yet.* Cf. *Princess,* concl. 52 :

> " our Britain, whole within herself,
> A nation yet," etc.

154, 155. *Thank him,* etc. This couplet is not in the 1st ed.

157. *Of boundless love and reverence.* The 1st ed. has " Of most unbounded reverence," etc. It does not contain line 159.

166. *For saving that, ye help to save mankind.* The 1st ed. reads : " For saving that, ye save mankind ; " in 168 : " And help the march of human mind ; " and in 169 : " Till crowds be sane and crowns be just."

170. *But wink no more,* etc. After this line the 1st ed. has the following, omitted in all subsequent eds. :

> " Perchance our greatness will increase ;
> Perchance a darkening future yields
> Some reverse from worse to worse,
> The blood of men in quiet fields,
> And sprinkled on the sheaves of peace."

It goes on thus :

> " And O remember him who led your hosts ;
> Respect his sacred warning ; guard your coasts ;
> His voice is silent," etc.

181–185. *Who let . . . a foe.* These five lines are not in the 1st ed., which goes on with " His eighty winters," etc.

195–217. *He on whom . . . and sun.* This fine passage is unaltered from the 1st ed. On the last line, cf. *Rev.* xxi. 23.

218. *Such was he,* etc. The 1st ed. reads :

> " He has not fail'd ; he hath prevail'd :
> So let the men whose hearths he saved from shame
> Thro' many and many an age proclaim
> At civic revel," etc.

241. *Ours the pain*, etc.   The line is not in the 1st ed.
251. *We revere*, etc.   The 1st ed. reads thus:

> " For solemn, too, this day are we.
> O friends, we doubt not that for one so true
> There must be other nobler work to do
> Than when he fought at Waterloo,
> And Victor he must ever be.
> Though worlds on worlds in myriad myriads roll
> Round us," etc.

252. *The tides*, etc.   The music at the funeral service in the cathedral.
266–270. *On God . . . dust to dust.*   These lines are not in the 1st ed.
271. *He is gone.*   The 1st ed. has "The man is gone;" and in 278, " But speak no more," etc.

INDEX OF WORDS AND PHRASES EXPLAINED.

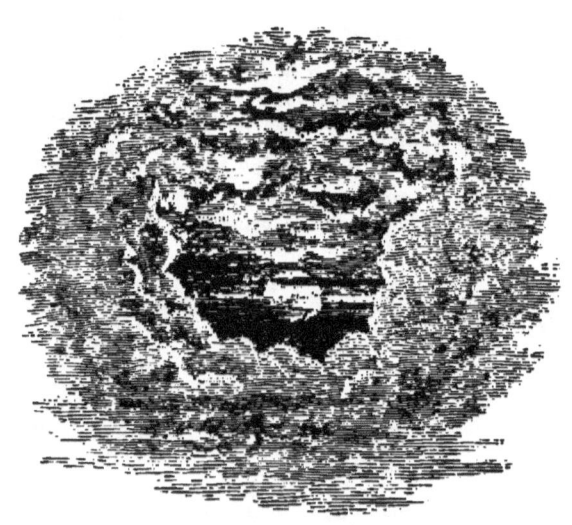

www.ingramcontent.com/pod-product-compliance
Lightning Source LLC
Chambersburg PA
CBHW031103020726
47495CB00007B/2030